PROJECT MERCURY

PROJECT MERCURY

RONALD L. SMITH

Clarion Books
An Imprint of HarperCollinsPublishers

Library of Congress Control Number: 2023941848
ISBN 978-0-06-331855-7

Typography by Jessie Gang
24 25 26 27 28 LBC 5 4 3 2 1

First Edition

PROLOGUE

IKE
Mercury Army Base, Nevada

"Ike! Get down here! Ten-hut!"

Ike Pressure groaned and clamped his hands over his ears. His mom's voice was as loud as an air siren. He rolled over on his back and stared up at the ceiling. Where did the word *ten-hut* come from, anyway?

He fumbled for his phone on the nightstand: 7 a.m. On a Saturday, no less.

"*Ike!*" the voice came again, this time with the force of a sonic boom.

He hopped out of bed jackrabbit fast. Natalie Pressure was known for quick punishment, which usually meant being grounded or having his computer taken away. He didn't want that to happen. In fact, the reason he was so tired was because he had been up all night playing *Shadow Goons*, a new zombie apocalypse game. He'd almost made it to level ten before he fell asleep in front of the screen, which is not a good way to get proper rest. But it was too late now. He threw on the same pants and shirt as the day before and headed down the stairs.

He was hoping to get a whiff of bacon, but no such luck. Lately, his mom had been on a health-food kick, and he was the unfortunate victim. No pancakes—too much flour. No sausage—too much fat. God forbid a few slices of crispy bacon. The last few mornings, he'd been forced to try tofu cheese, plant-based sausage links, and some kind of green ooze she'd whipped up in a blender. It tasted like swamp water. Not that he'd ever had swamp water before, but he was sure it would be just as awful.

He sighed.

It was tough being a thirteen-year-old with a drill sergeant for a mom.

The past several weeks his mom had talked a lot about "living sustainably" and "being mindful of the planet." Ike wasn't really sure where she was coming from. She didn't usually talk like this. She was in the military and always had her feet on the ground, with no time for what Ike's dad called hippie-dippie stuff.

Ike was an army brat, born in Georgia at Fort Moore Hospital. Most civilians thought that the word *brat* was an insult. Actually, it meant *privileged*. Like having the opportunity to travel all over the world at a young age. But it also meant going through a lot of stuff most kids didn't have to worry about. Things like dealing with a parent's long absence when they're deployed in an active war zone.

They were stationed in Georgia for five years, which is a long time for the army. His parents told him they could have gone to another base, but they had the option to stay because he was a baby.

After that, moving all the time was never fun. Ike was always the new kid in school, trying to readjust and make friends all over again. Which was hard because he was kind of shy. After traveling the globe for so long, he was glad that his mother was finally serving stateside.

Now here they were in Mercury, Nevada, where Ike's mom worked on the Mercury Army Base as a US Army Specialist. Ike wasn't exactly sure what a "specialist" did. She must have explained it to him once, but he didn't remember. His dad's job was easy to understand. He was in charge of new army recruits. It was his mission to design the programs that new soldiers had to master before getting out of basic training. He once showed Ike a video where young men and women climbed ropes, crawled through muddy ditches, ran in the blazing sun, and did fifty push-ups. All while being timed by a stopwatch. Ike almost threw up just watching it. He hated physical activity.

He hadn't enrolled in school yet since it was summer,

and he wasn't looking forward to it. Most kids would have been psyched to meet up with friends during summer break, but he didn't know anyone at Mercury Army Base Middle School yet. In fact, he hadn't met anyone in the few weeks that they had been here. He'd seen some kids his age around base housing riding bikes and playing sports, but hadn't gotten up the courage to introduce himself. What was the point, he often thought. Before too long, there'd be another move, and his family would be stationed in some far-flung destination once again.

Ike pulled a chair back from the kitchen table and sat down. His mother's nose was buried in a word-search book, one of her morning rituals.

"Where's Dad?" he asked.

"He had to go in this morning," she replied, not looking up.

The toaster dinged, and Ike got up to retrieve a slice. "Ow!" he cried, tossing the hot bread onto a plate. He sat back down. The toast looked as dry as the Nevada desert. He scanned the table for jelly, peanut butter, anything. "Uh," he started. "No jam?"

"Too much sugar," his mom replied.

Ike sighed and reached for a pitcher of fresh-squeezed orange juice. Sugar-free, of course. His mom smiled, revealing gleaming white teeth. She wore glasses, like Ike, and her hair was exactly 4.0 inches long, just above her earlobes and the collar of her uniform. The military had so many rules, Ike's head spun whenever he was reminded of them—which was often. Like every other military boy, he got a buzz cut every few weeks. "High and tight," his father would always tell the barber, as the old guy hovered over him with the clippers. Ike would shrink in the chair, trying to will himself to disappear. He didn't like getting haircuts and wanted to grow out an Afro, but his dad said he couldn't do it until he graduated from high school. If that day ever came, Ike often thought. It seemed an eternity away.

Everything having to do with the military was about regulations—from haircuts to lawn care. One time, Ike saw his dad bend down and measure the grass with a ruler. *A ruler.* It was the most "military" thing he'd ever seen him do. Except for that one time when he threatened to make Ike clean the bathroom with a toothbrush. It was only to prove a point—that Ike wasn't keeping his room clean—and he stopped him as soon as he got down on his knees to begin scrubbing.

Ike chewed and swallowed the dry toast and washed it down with orange juice. "Gotta go," he said. "Doing some more exploring today."

His mom finally looked up from her book. "Oh, really?

Don't go too far, Ike. You don't know your way around yet. Why not wait for your father to come home, and you can explore together?"

Ike didn't want to wait. There was nobody he'd rather be with than himself. "Uh," he started. "Well, I kind of want to go on my own."

His mom leaned back in her chair and crossed her arms. She shook her head, but a smile played along her lips. "You know what we used to call you when you were little?"

"No," he groaned.

"Little Mr. Play-Alone. You always wanted to be by yourself. That's why we were so happy when you and Eesha became best friends."

Ike shuddered.

"Well," he said, "we were kind of *forced* to play together."

His mother scoffed. "Aw, it wasn't *that* bad now, was it?"

Yes, Mom. It was that bad.

Ike's and Eesha's families had been stationed on the same military base back in Georgia. In fact, both families had lived on the same block. That wasn't the issue, though. The problem was that everyone thought that Ike and Eesha were destined to become lifelong friends because they were born on the same day. Ike thought that was absolutely ridiculous. Even at five years old, he knew they didn't really get along. He thought Eesha was loud and rude, and she probably thought he was too quiet and nerdy. Or worse. But that was all in the past now. He barely remembered her.

"You go ahead, Mr. Play-Alone," his mom said. "Just be back in a few hours for lunch."

Ike wondered what lunch would be. Something healthy, obviously.

☆ ☆ ☆

Every time Ike's family moved to a new base, he did all kinds of research on where they were headed. Mercury, Nevada, was no exception. It was about sixty-five miles northwest of Las Vegas and closed to outsiders, which wasn't unusual. Most bases were like that, except for a few people who worked in fast-food restaurants or other retail jobs. But the weird thing about Mercury was that back in the 1960s, they tested a lot of nuclear bombs at a place called the Nevada Test Site.

Ike knew there had to be some kind of big military secrets they were hiding. In fact, the base was closed years ago but had recently opened back up, and military families were being assigned there once again. He found that a little strange. When his mom and dad drove him around the army base the day they first arrived, he saw ominous gray buildings everywhere with giant signs that read:

WARNING
RESTRICTED AREA
USE OF DEADLY FORCE AUTHORIZED

Ike wondered what all the secrecy was about. His ideas ranged from supersonic future weapons to fallout shelters in case of nuclear attack. He really wanted to explore the buildings, but he knew, growing up in a military family, that rules were rules. Period. But still, it bugged him that he didn't know. *I'll find out one day*, he told himself.

He drained his glass of orange juice and went back upstairs to grab his backpack. A minute later he was headed out the door. "Ike!" his mom shouted. "Don't let the door bang shut!"

The door banged shut.

Although Nevada was mostly all desert, fourteen percent of the state was forest. And part of that wooded refuge was right through Ike's back door. When he went for his walks, he used an app on his phone to find out what kind of trees he was looking at. He discovered pines and Douglas firs, their long limbs soaring to the sky; and lots of interesting-looking shrubs and cacti, also called succulents.

When they first moved to Mercury, his parents took him to Great Basin National Park, where he saw one of the oldest living trees in the world. It was called the bristlecone pine and was over four thousand years old!

Ike always felt good in the forest. It was one of his favorite things to do. He always imagined he was on an adventure, like a character from one of the fantasy books he liked to read. Sometimes, he'd find the perfect fallen tree branch to use as a staff. A magical one, of course, that could bring a streak of blue lightning down from the sky and vanquish all his enemies.

He wiped his brow. It was hot out, the middle of June. A fly buzzed in his ear and he swatted it away. He wasn't looking for anything particular, but he always found something of interest. A few days before, he'd stumbled upon a giant white mushroom. We're talking *giant*, like ten inches around. The bottom had those weird accordion-like ridges, but they were *green*! Ike looked it up and discovered that the ridges were called gills. He took a picture of it with his phone and added it to what he called *Ike's Journal of Amazing and Fascinating Things*. It was just a folder on his computer, but one day he hoped to print it all out and turn it into a book.

He continued to walk, taking his time and enjoying the fresh air. Birds chirped and tweeted in the trees, jumping from branch to branch. The earth here was red, like clay. Ike bent down and scooped up a handful. He studied it closely, as if he were one of those old-timey prospectors panning for gold. He blew it out of his hand, and it settled back to earth in a huge cloud, staining his white sneakers a dusty red.

The sun was more intense now without the shade of the trees, and Ike felt sweat running down his back. *Should have brought a canteen of water*, he thought, remembering that his dad had given him one a long time ago. His mom and dad had all kinds of military stuff in a footlocker down in the basement: there were MREs, which stood for "meals ready to eat"; a gas mask, which he used to wear as a kid while running around the house; a folded American flag; a green tent with mosquito netting; a compass; and a bunch of maps. He found the maps fascinating and had a hard time believing that his mom and dad had grown up without cell phones and had to decipher them to get anywhere. That was totally bizarre!

Sometimes, when he was bored, he'd use the things from the footlocker as props for imaginary adventures, usually having to do with surviving a zombie apocalypse. If the day ever did come, he'd be prepared. Or at least that's what he liked to believe.

He hiked on, venturing farther from his back door than he usually did. He read that there were a lot of old arrowheads in Nevada, but he wasn't sure where to find them. He made a mental note to do more research on the subject when he got back home. Supposedly, there were old dinosaur bones around, too. Years ago, right here in this part of Nevada, someone had found the fossilized bones of an ichthyosaur, a type of prehistoric sea creature. Its skeleton was almost fifty feet long! Ike wondered what it must have been like to see that for the first time. Whoever had dug it up must have totally freaked out!

He slowed his steps. He was tired. And with the sun blazing down on him, he felt like he might pass out. Last night's marathon gaming session was catching up to him. His mom was definitely going to tell him to take a shower. But when he finally made it back home, dripping with sweat, she was beaming.

"Uh," he started. "What's going on with you?"

She rested her elbows on the table and propped her chin in her hands. "I have the best news," she said.

Ike's stomach flopped. One time she told him she had good news, and he ended up painting the inside of the garage.

"What?" he asked nervously.

"The Webbs," she replied with glee. "Eesha and her family are moving to Mercury! Isn't that exciting?"

Ike suddenly felt like he was in a movie, where the camera slowly zooms in on the main character's face for a shocked close-up. *It couldn't be. With all the military bases in the world, she had to come here, to Mercury, Nevada?*

He groaned.

"Ike?" his mom ventured. "Ike to Earth."

"Yeah?"

"Isn't that exciting?" she said again. "You'll be able to play together, just like when you were little. It'll be so much fun!" She sat back and smiled. "Did I ever tell you about the time when you were both in diapers and—"

"Mom!" Ike shouted.

His mother shot him a side-eye.

"Do not raise your voice in this house, Ike Pressure. Do you understand?"

He pushed his glasses up on his nose. "Yes, ma'am."

Natalie Pressure waited a beat before continuing, letting her last command sink in. "Now, I have to run some errands. I'll be back soon, okay?"

"Okay," he relented.

Once his mother left the room, Ike let out an exhausted breath.

Eesha, he thought.

It had been eight years since he had last seen her in Georgia. She was probably worse now than when they were kids.

He swallowed the lump in his throat.

"Don't forget lunch," his mom called as she headed out the door. "I left some soy hot dogs for you!"

Great, Ike thought. *Just fantastic.*

EESHA
Jim Sawyer Army Base, Illinois

Eesha Webb took another gulp of nuclear-red fruit punch.

"Buurrpp!"

"Ew!" two voices echoed at the same time. "Gross!"

The chorus came from Jack and Jill Webb, Eesha's six-year-old twin siblings. She called them nerd-bots.

"I'm telling Mom!" Jack threatened her. "She said burping's . . . not nice!"

"Yeah!" Jill chimed in. "You're a . . . you're a rude-butt!"

In answer, Eesha let out another burp.

Both kids scrambled out of the room, frantically shouting for their mother. Eesha laughed. *Could they be any more goofy?* she thought.

She took off before the twins returned, out the back door and onto her bike. She sped down the street, pedaling as fast as she could. Her mom would give her a lecture when she got back, but Eesha didn't care about that at the moment. She knew her mom was a softie. Eesha knew just what to do to appear sorry. She'd stick out her bottom lip until it trembled, promise she wouldn't burp in front of the twins again, and then give her mom a hug. It worked every time. Dad, on the other hand, was no sucker for Eesha's antics, which is why she never acted out in front of him.

Eesha raised her head up to the sun as she rode, letting the warm rays bathe her face. She took her hands off the handlebars and spread her arms wide, enjoying the sense of freedom. It felt wonderful. She had no destination in mind, she just wanted to ride. Somehow, she ended up near the main gate. She came to a stop, winded, and studied the guard in the little booth. She was an MP, which stood for military police. It was her job to check the IDs of everyone coming onto the base.

Eesha looked past the little guardhouse and into the distance. *Civilians* were out there. She wondered what it would be like to zip by the guard and take off into the wild blue yonder. She'd go on an adventure! She'd ride down unknown streets and meet new kids. Buy sneakers at a different mall. Eat cheeseburgers at a new fast-food restaurant. But it was all a fantasy. Kids weren't allowed off base without their parents' approval. She'd be in a heap of trouble if she ever tried something like that.

More than anything, Eesha wanted to get away from Jim Sawyer Army Base. According to her, it was the Most Boring Place in the World. She needed adventure. Not the typical camping trip or school outing, but *real* adventure, like in *Amazing Jane*, a graphic novel she'd been reading. Amazing Jane was only fourteen, but in the book, she'd stopped a crime ring in Amsterdam, received the Medal of Freedom for foiling a terrorist threat, and still had time to be a rock star! A drummer, no less, in a band called the Ladybugs!

Now *that* was adventure.

Eesha watched as the guard picked up a pair of binoculars.

And pointed them her way.

She gulped. *I'm not doing anything wrong. Just looking.* But she didn't feel like being questioned by the MP, so she turned her bike around and took off.

☆ ☆ ☆

Back home, Eesha was in for a surprise. Not only was her mom in the living room with the twins, but her dad was there, too.

She glanced at the clock on the wall. It was noon. What was Dad doing home so early?

"Eesha," her mom started.

Eesha gulped and looked at the nerd-bots. *Little tattletales!*

"Sit down, honey," her dad said in his best drill instructor voice.

Now she *was* worried. What kind of trouble was she in?

Her mother caught her stare, like a deer in headlights. "I've got good news," she said, "and bad. What do you want to hear first?"

Eesha's right hand flew up to her mouth to chew a fingernail, a habit she was trying to break, without much success. "Um, bad?" she ventured.

"You're grounded," her dad immediately announced. The twins clapped.

Eesha bolted up from her seat. She shot eye daggers at the twins, who seemed to be enjoying the spectacle. "For what?" she complained. "For burping? C'mon, Dad!"

"Burping?" her mom repeated, dumbfounded. "No, it's not for that, but thanks for telling us."

Eesha closed her eyes in resignation. Jack and Jill snickered and made faces.

"It's for leaving the twins unattended," her mom clarified. "I've told you about that before. You are not to leave this house without telling me or your father where you're going!"

Eesha opened her eyes and sat back down. She was definitely on The List now. She didn't know what The List was, but her mom and dad had threatened her with it more times than she could count.

"Your mother's right," her father added. "We've told you this before, Eesha. Over and over."

She looked up and attempted the trembling-lip move.

"Don't even try it," her father warned.

She wilted.

"But," her mother said, holding up a finger. "We've got good news, too."

Eesha raised her head, hopeful. What could it be? A new bike? Her own laptop? *Oh my god. They're going to let me get that drum kit I've always wanted!*

But it was nothing of the sort.

"We're moving," her mom announced, and looked at her husband, who took her hand. "Daddy just got his transfer papers!"

Eesha's eyes lit up. "Moving? Where? When?"

"In a few weeks," her father replied. "Still a lot to sort out first. You know the military. They make you fill out paperwork just to go to the bathroom!"

He laughed a little too loudly, and then looked to his wife for agreement. She ignored him.

Finally, Eesha thought. *We're getting out of this boring place!*

Maybe they'd be moving to Japan, she hoped, being a big fan of manga. Or Germany or France!

"So?" she asked, excited now, her knee pumping up and down like a piston. "Where are we going?"

"A little place called Mercury, Nevada," her mother said.

Silence.

"Nevada?" she finally replied, tilting her head. The word felt funny in her mouth. She didn't know too much about Nevada. It was a lot of desert, she knew that much. And it was near New Mexico. They'd never lived in the Southwest before, she realized. Actually, it might be kind of cool. "Great," she said. "Sounds like fun."

Mrs. Webb looked at her daughter and smiled. "Best of all, we'll be on the same base as our old friends, Natalie Pressure and her family. You can see Ike again!"

Eesha's smile froze on her face.

Ike Pressure.

He'd have to be a full-blown nerd by now.

Eesha's parents thought that she and Ike shared some kind of special destiny because they were born on the same day on the same army base. But Eesha had nothing in common with him. Except that they were forced to play together when they were little.

"Isn't that great?" her dad exclaimed. "The birthday kids ride again!"

Eesha closed her eyes.

What did I do to deserve this?

Chapter One

It didn't take long for the Webb and Pressure families to meet up for their reunion. Ike wasn't looking forward to it.

The designated meeting spot was a picnic area a few miles from the army base. Other than the trip to the Great Basin, it was the first time he'd been off base in Mercury.

Military bases are self-contained universes. Everything a family could ever need was right there. A grocery store—called a commissary; the PX, which stood for post exchange, similar to a Walgreens or Rite Aid but with more stuff, like clothes, appliances, and the like. There were even McDonald's and other fast-food restaurants. But it was all contained within the base's perimeter.

When people talked about military bases, there were two things to remember. People lived on base housing, which was like any neighborhood, except for all the houses looking the same, and then there was the installation itself—where military personnel worked—also called the base. So, if someone said they were going to the base, they were talking about the military installation. But at the same time, you *lived* on the base. But not where people worked. Confusing. But that was the military. Standard operating procedure.

On the way to the picnic area, Ike peered out the window. The natural landscape was beautiful with red mountains and stony cliffs in the distance. Large birds wheeled in a blue sky. He wondered what it was like hundreds of years ago. It must have been unspoiled. No plastic bottles on the side of the road. No *roads*, for that matter. Clean, sparkling rivers and lakes. Buffalo grazing on the plains. Ike felt sad when he thought about how people treated the Earth now. Humans were awful. Now there was pollution and trash everywhere, and it was getting worse every day.

At the picnic area, Ike's dad unloaded a cooler full of cold drinks and all the fixings for burgers and hot dogs. His mom had made her special potato salad and lemonade. Ike had to admit, he *was* looking forward to eating. His mom had agreed to a special food "cheat day," probably because she knew his dad wouldn't want to eat soy dogs or tofu burgers on a day like this—a reunion with his old basketball buddy, where they would reminisce about sports and whatever other boring stuff dads talked about.

Ike leaned back in one of their green-and-yellow lounge chairs. A few other families were opening car trunks and setting up supplies. Ike saw a little boy and his dad inspecting their fishing rods. Ike didn't like fishing. Actually, he'd never even *been* fishing. The thought of hooking a fish inside its mouth seemed really cruel to him. At least some people threw them back in the water. His dad liked to fish, but had never asked him to go. Ike often wondered how his dad really felt about him. He was pretty sure he had wanted his son to be like him—into sports and manly stuff—but that wasn't Ike. At all.

It was a beautiful day for a cookout. Their table was near the edge of the woods, where trees provided some shade from the Nevada heat. A slight wind stirred in the treetops. Ike was nervous, wondering what it would be like to see Eesha again after all this time. He tried to tell himself it wouldn't be too bad, but deep down, he knew it probably would be.

He wiped a hand across his sweating forehead. People said that Nevada was supposed to have dry heat, whatever that meant. To Ike, it was just hot. His mom had told him to put on one of his dad's baseball caps, but Ike didn't like wearing them. *They make me look dorky*, he'd told her several times.

"Here you go, champ," his father said, pulling a soda

from the cooler. "Pretty hot out here today."

Ike took the drink and raised it to his lips. It felt good going down, and he almost drank it all in one long gulp. He wanted to burp, but he knew his parents wouldn't approve. "Thanks," he offered instead.

His dad wore a white polo shirt, khaki shorts, and military issue sunglasses. His shorts were way too high on his waist. If there were a magazine called *Dorky Military Dads*, he'd be one of the models. His biceps were like boulders, though. He once told Ike that he was a champion wrestler in college and almost went pro. Ike wasn't sure what pro wrestling was really like. The only wrestlers he'd ever seen were the guys on TV in weird outfits and masks who threw each other around the ring like cartoon characters. He certainly couldn't imagine his father doing that.

Ike heard his mother sigh. She glanced at her watch and wrinkled her brow. "I told them to be here at 1300 hours."

"Maybe they had car trouble or something," Ike's dad put in. He already had the grill going, and the smell of cooking meat made Ike's mouth water. His dad stood over the flames like a cooking general, a spatula in one hand and a mitt on the other.

Ike knew that 1300 hours meant 1 p.m. military time. It was based on the 24-hour clock and was easy to remember. Noon was 1200 hours, 1 p.m. was 1300 hours, 2 p.m.

was 1400 hours, and so on and so forth until you got to midnight, which was zero hour and looked like this: 0000.

Ike had absolutely no idea why the military had its own time system.

He took another sip of soda, then whipped out his phone and tried to log onto *Shadow Goons* but couldn't get a signal. He sighed.

"I see a car," his mom called out hopefully.

Ike shaded his eyes with the edge of his hand. A giant black SUV was slowly approaching, its huge tires crunching over the small rock-and-gravel path that led up to the picnic area. *Why do they have to be so big?* he asked himself. *Ozone-destroying dinosaurs.*

"That's them!" his mom shouted with glee. Ike slowly got up and followed his parents to the vehicle.

The big SUV pulled up next to them in a cloud of red dust. The window came down with a hiss, and a blast of cool air wafted out. Mr. Webb was wearing aviator sunglasses and chewing a toothpick. He smiled, revealing gleaming white teeth. "I'm looking for a man who thinks he can play basketball but ain't got no game," he said around his toothpick.

Ike jumped as an explosion of laughter cut through the hot air. The doors flew open and the Webbs poured out. While Ike's mom and dad hugged and clapped their old friends on the back, two kids scrambled from the back seat. Jack and Jill, Ike's mom had said. Twins. They hadn't been born yet the last time he saw Eesha. They didn't speak, only stared at him like he had three heads.

The rear door opened on the other side. And then, as Ike held his breath, Eesha Webb unfolded her long limbs from the back seat.

She was taller than him, perhaps by a few inches at least. Her hair was long, bunched up into little braided buns on her head. Ike noticed the green high-top sneakers and blue gym shorts, as if she had just come from playing basketball. Her shirt read: JIM SAWYER ARMY BASE GAZELLES.

For a moment they just stared at each other. Ike didn't know what to say. It was almost like a standoff. He suddenly came to a decision. He had to be polite. At least try. His parents were expecting them to get along. He let out a nervous breath and pushed his glasses up on his nose.

"Hi," he said.

Eesha cracked her neck to the side, like she was warming up for a fight, but instead returned the greeting.

"Hey, dork. What's up?"

Chapter Two

Ike stood there.

Frozen.

He felt a trickle of sweat on his forehead, which he was sure was making its way down his cheek to settle in the corner of his eye. He wiped it away.

"Aw, I'm just kidding!" Eesha said, and punched him on the shoulder. *Hard.*

Ike faked a chuckle. He wanted to rub his arm, but he couldn't let her know how much her punch actually *hurt*. God, she was tall. They stood there for a moment, not saying anything at all. Ike shuffled his feet, tongue-tied.

"You haven't changed much," she said, which sounded like an insult. "Still wearing glasses. I used to call you Four-Eyes. Remember?"

Ike certainly did remember. It was one of her *nicer* nicknames.

"Kids!" Ike's dad called out. "Get over here. We're gonna eat!"

Ike was glad for the interruption because he didn't have a comeback.

They made their way over to the picnic tables. The twins were already seated, both of them guzzling lemonade like they were dying of thirst. Ike's mom and dad looked as happy as he had ever seen them, all big smiles and crazy laughter. His dad had already pressed play on his old-school boom box, and corny R&B music filled the air. Eesha trailed behind Ike as if she didn't want to follow. Ike felt embarrassed.

It was going to be a long day.

Mr. Webb clapped Ike on the shoulder as he sat down. It felt like a hammer blow from John Henry, a folk hero he'd read about in school. *Jeez! What is it with these people hitting everyone!*

"Looks like you've gained a few inches, Ike," he said, still gnawing on his toothpick. Ike was surprised it hadn't been chewed to splinters yet. "How's your basketball game going? Eesha's gonna try out for varsity next year."

"Uh," Ike started. "I'm not really into sports that much."

Eesha leaned back and crossed her arms. *God*, Ike thought. *She has better muscles than me.*

"Ike spends a lot of time exploring," his mother put in. "Collecting rocks and things. Maybe he'll be a geologist or something like that one day. Right, Ike?"

Ike gave a noncommittal nod but smiled inside. His mom was actually sticking up for him. Not everyone was into sports like Eesha.

"Rocks?" Eesha said in a dismissive tone. Ike wanted to disappear.

"I think that's great," Eesha's mom said, as if congratulating a child on a simple achievement. "Not just anyone can be a pro athlete." She glanced at Ike. "These kids have their whole lives in front of them, Natalie. I'm sure they'll figure it all out. Take me, for example. I didn't know I wanted to be an army engineer until I was finished with college." She paused. "At *West Point*."

For a moment, Ike thought he caught his mother rolling her eyes.

The Webbs seemed like a family of competitors. Ike wasn't competitive at all. He hated gym class and anything more strenuous than a hike. One time, a PE teacher named Mr. Sofio tried to make him climb the rope. Try as he might, he just couldn't do it. Chin-ups were also torture. Ike *hated* sports. Maybe one day, he'd find his passion and excel at it. Perhaps he could be a video game designer or work in movies doing special effects. Now *that* would be cool.

He got up and made a beeline for the grill. After getting

a burger and bun, he loaded it up with mustard, onions, ketchup, and a little bit of mayo. *Finally*, he thought. *Something that tastes good.*

Eesha eyed him as he brought his meal back to the table. She sipped from a red water bottle. "Are you gonna eat anything?" he asked.

Eesha snorted. "Gotta watch my calorie intake. I'm in training."

"Right," Ike replied, and then thought: *How boring.*

He bit into the burger. Juice and ketchup dripped down his chin, and he didn't hesitate to lick his fingers, even though he knew it was kind of gross.

While their parents talked and laughed, the twins found a set of nearby swings and were keeping themselves busy, soaring precariously high. No one seemed to notice.

"So," Eesha said. "What's there to do around here?"

Ike shrugged. "I play a lot of video games. Do some exploring in the woods."

"Ah," Eesha replied. "I figured you'd be into gaming."

He rattled off the names of a bunch of fantasy role-playing games, but Eesha didn't recognize any of them.

"Most of the stuff I play is sports stuff," she told him. "Ever heard of *SpeedRunners* or *Champion Jump Ball*?"

"Nope," Ike replied.

"*Blitz Bowl*? *Marathon Speeder*?"

Ike shook his head.

An awkward silence filled the air between them. Eesha suddenly leaned in a little. Ike drew back. She looked left, right, and then lowered her voice. "Did you know that Area 51 is right here in Nevada?"

Ike gulped down another bite of his burger. "Area what?"

Eesha drew back, stunned. "You're not serious, are you? You've never heard of Area 51?"

"Nope."

They hadn't even been together twenty minutes yet, and he was already tired of her.

Eesha looked to her parents and then back to Ike. She lowered her voice again. "It's a secret military base in the desert. This base here in Mercury is probably connected to it. I've got a whole plan figured out for how to investigate."

"Uh," Ike replied skeptically. "Okay."

Eesha leaned forward. "Area 51 is all about UFOs and aliens. I read that they have actual alien bodies there!"

Ike was stunned. He had a vivid imagination, but he didn't think any of the stuff in the sci-fi books he'd read was true. He never would have taken Eesha for a conspiracy theorist.

"So," he began cautiously, almost as a joke. "What's your plan?"

Eesha smiled, and Ike saw that her front teeth, which used to be stained red from drinking too much fruit punch, were now white and bright. She stared at Ike a moment, and then, in the most serious voice ever, whispered, "I'm going to find out if UFOs and aliens . . . are *real*!"

Chapter Three

Ike raced up to his room the moment they arrived home. He flipped open his laptop and started his search:

Area 51 aliens UFOs

He got so many results, he didn't know where to begin. But, like the expert researcher he was, he dove in.

Three hours later, he closed the laptop and rubbed his bleary eyes. How did he not know about all this? There were a ton of websites about UFOs and aliens, most of them centering around Roswell, New Mexico, where, allegedly, a spacecraft crashed in 1947. The air force covered it up, but numerous witnesses over the years had come forward with odd tales. One of them said they had found a piece of metal that was as light as a sheet of paper but stronger than iron. It also had strange hieroglyphic-like writing on it. Another said that dead alien bodies were taken from the spaceship and flown to Wright-Patterson Air Force Base in Ohio for autopsies. There was even a story about how the president at that time, Harry S. Truman, made a pact with the aliens: if they gave us their technology, we would allow them to take and study humans! That's how we got fiber optics, lasers, and transistors!

Ike sat back and took another sip of lukewarm lemonade. His head was spinning. The Mercury Army Base was in the middle of nowhere. And not far away was the Nevada Test Site, where they used to test nuclear bombs. What else was going on in the desert? There had to be more to it. Could Eesha be right about all of this?

Of course not.

It was all a bunch of conspiracy theory stuff.

He chuckled. *Can't believe I fell down that rabbit hole.*

Later that night though, when he finally fell asleep after watching every video he could find on the subject, he dreamed of UFOs and bug-eyed aliens.

☆ ☆ ☆

The next night at dinner, Ike moved the mashed potatoes and baked salmon around on his plate. He wasn't hungry. His father was on his second piece of salmon already. "Mashed potatoes," he said, licking his lips. "My favorite."

Ike had to admit the potatoes were good, even though they were made with soy milk and some kind of weird fake butter.

All day, against his better judgment, he'd been obsessed with Eesha's stories and the stuff he'd found online. When he was researching, he'd discovered something called Project Blue Book, which was a top secret military organization that was all about studying UFOs. Is that why they moved here? Was his mom working on something secret? If he started asking questions, she might get suspicious and blow her cover. Ike paused. *Blow your cover.* That's what they always said in spy movies. He let out a breath.

"Mom?"

"Yes, honey?"

"What's your job on the base, anyway?"

Ike's mother shot her husband a quick glance before looking to Ike. "Oh. Well, what brings this up?"

Ike speared a single green pea with his fork. "You never told me. I was just curious."

"You know what they say about curiosity, right, Ike?" his father asked.

"No."

"That it killed the cat!" his dad practically shouted.

Dad jokes, Ike thought, shaking his head. *Okay, boomer.*

His parents laughed. Sometimes Ike didn't understand their old-timey jokes and sayings. He just gave his father a blank stare. "What does that mean?"

"That being nosy can get you in trouble," his dad told him.

"I'm not being nosy," Ike shot back.

His mother smiled. "Oh, honey, we know." She looked briefly to her husband again and then back to Ike. "So. I'm what they call a specialist."

Ike nodded. "Right. But what are you a specialist *at*?"

Natalie Pressure dabbed the corners of her mouth with a napkin. "Strategic initiatives, they call them. Also, intelligence systems and threat identification. Does that explain it for you?"

"Uh, not really." *Was she being secretive?*

"Let's just say I'm helping to keep the nation safe and leave it at that," she finished.

Ike looked to his father, whose face had suddenly gone serious. But he had nothing to add.

☆ ☆ ☆

It wasn't long before Ike and Eesha met up again. This time, it was a dinner at Eesha's house. At first, Ike complained. He really didn't feel like going. He wanted to stay home and finish the next level in *Shadow Goons*. He had a whole horde of zombies to knock out before they attacked a band of survivors. But then he realized it would be a good chance to find out more about Eesha's suspicions. And his own.

He knew they could have walked to the Webbs', but his father liked his new black Audi sedan so much, they drove instead. Ike sunk into the supple leather back seat and put his earbuds in. Recently, he had discovered classical music. The combination of instruments—woodwinds, strings, percussion, and horns—helped his imagination run wild. While the music played, he saw fiery explosions and heroic warriors. No wonder so many movies used this kind of music for soundtracks. He even found a classical composer named Chevalier de Saint-Georges that he liked. They called him the Black Mozart. Ike thought that was lame. Why couldn't he be famous in his own right?

"We're here," his dad's voice cut through the music in his earbuds. He released a sigh and climbed out of the car. The doors shut with a resounding thud.

Ike followed his parents into the Webbs' house. It was laid out the same as theirs. Most base housing was modeled on the same blueprint: a living room and kitchen on the ground floor, two bedrooms and bathrooms upstairs, and a basement. A big-screen TV took up most of one living room wall. Some baseball game was on, loud as a stadium full of fans. Mrs. Webb walked to the foot of the stairs and shouted, "Eesha! Ike's here."

Ike shoved his hands into his pockets. The twins came thundering down like elephants. They ran up to him.

"Are you Eesha's boyfriend?" Jill asked.

"Yeah," Jack put in. "Are you gonna get married?"

Ike's stomach lurched. He felt as if he were suddenly on display. His palms were sweaty. *Were* they on a date or something? He took a moment to study the twins. Their fingers were stained bright red, and their mouths too. *Little beasts.* What could they have eaten to get that result? Some kind of fluorescent candy?

"*Children*," Eesha's mother scolded them, and they scurried away, giggling. Ike breathed a sigh of relief. A moment later Eesha came down the stairs, dressed in gym shorts and a T-shirt again. She gave Ike the universal head nod, and he returned it.

Everyone was gathered in the living room. Ike's dad was already sitting in front of the game, leaning forward, legs wide apart. Manspreading, people called it. Mr. Webb was gnawing his toothpick again, placing coasters on the table. Mrs. Webb was all smiles, but it seemed fake to Ike. He really didn't like her.

"You kids go entertain yourselves," she said to Ike and Eesha. "You two used to be inseparable! You said you were going to get married one day!"

Ike closed his eyes in embarrassment.

"C'mon," Eesha said. "Let's go."

She led him through the kitchen and into the backyard.

They stepped around a mountain of toys and starter bikes on the lawn. He followed her to a weathered picnic table, where they took seats across from each other. The sun was still strong, and Ike felt it scorching the back of his neck. He wondered if he'd ever get used to the Nevada heat.

"How long do you think that's gonna last?" Eesha asked him.

"What?"

She crossed her arms. "The whole 'when you were kids' thing. It's all they ever talk about."

"I know. It's so cringe."

For a moment, there was silence, except for the squawking of birds in the trees. They really didn't know each other at all. The twins crashed through the back door and ran around the yard in circles like wild children.

"So," Ike started, "I looked up some of the stuff you were talking about. Area 51 and all that. Do you really think our parents are stationed here to work on aliens and UFOs?"

Eesha gave a slight grin. "Not mine. They both have boring jobs where they sit at computers all day long studying conflict zones."

"But how do you know that's true?" Ike challenged her.

His dad's job didn't seem very secretive at all. Now his *mom*, on the other hand: intelligence systems and threat identification? *That* sounded kind of mysterious.

"I know it's true," Eesha replied. "I snooped around on them a long time ago. Whatever base we're stationed at, they always do the same kind of work."

Ike rested his elbows on the table. "When I asked my mom what her job was, she just gave me some answer that really didn't mean anything. And then they both joked about curiosity killing the cat."

"Figures," Eesha replied. "Listen. I was thinking, the first thing we have to do is get onto the base and have a look around."

Ike almost laughed. "We?"

"I thought you were going to help."

"I never said that. Plus, um, you *do* know there are people with machine guns on the base, right? The military police?"

Eesha ignored him. "There has to be a way to get some information."

Ike couldn't believe it.

"Look," Eesha continued. "I just want to find out what's going on at the base. It could be something really mysterious."

Ike felt a little tingle of excitement. Maybe she was onto something. The sun passed behind a cloud, bringing a slight relief from the heat.

"*And,*" she went on, "your mom was definitely acting fishy when you asked what her job was."

She's right, Ike thought. *Maybe we could just do a little digging.* He liked adventures. At least in books. "Okay," he relented. "So, what do you think we should do?"

"That's what I'm talking about!" Eesha sprang up from her seat and raised her hand for a high five.

Ike awkwardly slapped her palm.

"So," she went on, sitting back down, getting more excited. "We both have military IDs, right? We can get past the gate if we show them. They'll think we're just going to the PX or something."

"True," Ike considered.

"Then we can have a look around, you know? Maybe we'll find something . . . I don't know. A clue."

"We could do it on bikes," Ike suggested.

"Yeah!" Eesha half shouted. "Just like in the movies. Like *E.T.* and *Stranger Things.* Kids on bikes always save the day!"

Ike burst out laughing before he could stop himself, but quickly regained his composure. "Cool. So, when do we do this?"

Eesha's eyes lit up. "No time like the present, they always say."

"Tomorrow?" Ike ventured.

"It's a date!" Eesha exclaimed, and then froze. Her mouth formed an O. "Um, I mean. Yeah. Let's, um . . . meet up."

Ike's embarrassment was interrupted by the sound of the back door flying open again. "Eesha!" Mrs. Webb shouted. "Ike! Get in here! We wanna see that dance you used to do when you were little!"

Chapter Four

Ike took his bike from the garage and wheeled it out to the driveway. He hadn't really done much riding since they'd arrived in Mercury. He liked his walks in the woods a bit more. For some reason, they gave him a sense of freedom that the bike couldn't. Maybe it was because he could stop and observe things: rocks, trees, mysterious plants, the local flora and fauna.

Breakfast had been a bowl of cereal. Not the sugary type, but something his mom had brought home called Great Grainy Goodness, which was supposed to be all-natural. If all-natural meant tasting like cardboard, they had achieved their goal.

He hopped on his bike and headed down the driveway. It was another brilliant day with puffy white clouds in a picture-book blue sky. Hopefully, he wouldn't be sweltering by the time he got to Eesha's. He took his time, checking out the houses and the few people out for morning jogs. He passed several people walking their dogs, lunging against their leashes to run alongside him. Ike loved dogs, but his parents said that he'd have to wait another year to get one. They said it was a big responsibility, and since they worked all the time, he'd have to be the one to take care of it. Ike already knew what kind of dog he wanted. Not some fancy breed, but a mutt from the shelter. Someone once told him that's where all the best dogs were.

Ike looked at street names as he passed them. Banshee. Washington. Mockingbird. They didn't seem to have any rhyme or reason to them. When they lived in Georgia, all of the names on base housing had tree names: Spruce, Elm, Cedar. They had lived on Rowan Street, which Ike thought was cool because that tree showed up in a lot of fantasy books. He looked it up once and discovered that it was used by ancient Druids for medicine and rituals.

After he passed the base swimming pool, he turned onto Eesha's street, which was called Gover. He had no idea who or what a Gover was. Eesha was waiting for him in her driveway. She had a cool bike, much newer than Ike's. It was mint green, with whitewall tires and front and back fenders. A sticker on the frame displayed the message *If you can read this, you're too close. Back off!*

Ike's bike was much more traditional, with a standard frame and high handlebars, painted basic black. His sticker read: *I Brake for Hobbits.*

"You made it," she said.

"Did you think I wouldn't?"

"I wasn't sure."

For a moment, Ike wondered if he'd made a mistake going along with Eesha on this. He was pretty sure there was nothing to discover on the base, but it was still an adventure.

"Ready?" she asked.

"Yup. Let's go."

The streets were easy to navigate without a lot of traffic. There just weren't too many cars on the road in base housing. They rode side by side on the broad street, taking in the sights. "Perfect weather," Ike said.

"Yeah. Wanna race?"

And there it is, Ike thought. *The competition*. He suddenly felt like he was in gym class.

"I guess," he relented. "If you really want to."

They both stopped pedaling. A large tree with heavy branches and leaves reached over the street, providing a little shade.

Eesha peered down the road. "See that red truck in that driveway down there?"

Ike looked and then nodded.

"One," Eesha began. "Two . . ."

A second later they were both hurtling to the end of

the block. Ike pumped his legs furiously, Eesha keeping pace with him. The red truck loomed closer. Ike was only a moment away. He glanced to his side. He was winning. Eesha lagged behind him by a tire length. He suddenly felt the need to win, to push himself, something he had never experienced before.

And that's when Eesha passed him, coasting to a stop with her arms off the handlebars and spread wide.

"Sucker!" she called.

Ike pulled up alongside her.

"Nice try, Pressure," she said. "Maybe next time."

"Sure," Ike said, winded.

Not.

Five minutes later, the main gate of the army base came into view.

"Got your ID?" Eesha asked.

"Yup."

"Okay, let's just ride up and say we're going to the PX."

"Sounds good," Ike replied.

Ike felt nervous as they approached. They weren't doing anything wrong, though. Military kids had access to the army base because they were the dependents of an adult who worked there.

Eesha pulled up to the gate first. Ike followed behind her. A moment later, a woman wearing a green uniform and a white helmet with *MP* stamped on the front stepped out of the little guardhouse. She wore sunglasses, and she wasn't smiling.

"Hi!" Eesha burst out. A little too excitedly.

The MP just stared. "ID."

Eesha reached into her back pocket and handed it to her. The MP took off her sunglasses and studied it. "Your purpose on the base?"

"Oh," Eesha started. "We're both new here. We just wanted to explore the PX. Maybe buy some video games or something."

The MP didn't reply. She handed the card back to Eesha, who maneuvered her bike out of the way a little so Ike could come up next.

"ID, please."

Ike was already holding it, and he handed it to her. The MP looked at the card, and then Ike. And then again, as if she was checking something. Ike swallowed.

"Pressure, huh?" she said. "Cool name."

"Oh," Ike said, relieved. "It's um. Yeah, thanks."

The MP handed the ID back. "I don't have to tell you to stay away from restricted areas, right?"

"Right," Eesha said.

"Well, have a good day," the MP said.

"Thanks," Ike replied.

The crossing gate rose up, and Ike and Eesha passed through.

☆ ☆ ☆

Every building was beige, white, or army green. They passed an airfield, where massive planes sat like giant metallic beasts. Workers carried huge boxes of some kind of cargo from plane to plane on handcarts. Ike had no idea what it could be. Weapons of some sort?

"Those planes are probably going to conflict zones," Eesha said. "That's what my dad told me."

Ike was glad that his mom and dad had yet to be deployed to a hot spot. He didn't think he would like that at all. "Where's the PX?" Eesha asked.

Ike didn't know, so they rode around and explored. Several buildings were marked with No Entry and Restricted Area signs. He had no idea where his mom worked. She could be in any one of these buildings right now.

They pedaled along, checking them out. Jeeps rumbled by, their drivers offering friendly waves. New recruits worked out in a wide expanse of green lawn to their left. He wondered if they really knew what they had signed up for. He could hear the drill instructor berating them in the loudest voice he'd ever heard. Ike felt tired just looking at them.

Eesha was taking her time, pedaling slowly, looking at

everything they passed. Ike was wondering if their adventure was really nothing more than a little bike ride.

They found the PX easily enough because the base was only so big. Plus, there were military-issue green signs everywhere. They parked their bikes in a rack and went inside. Neither one of them had bike locks. That was one good thing about military bases: they were the safest and most law-abiding places to be found anywhere.

They roamed the aisles, looking for nothing in particular. Ike found the video game section, but they didn't have anything new, just games he already had. Eesha was going to buy a shirt that read: *Proud US Army Brat.*

"Hey," Ike whispered to her as she flipped through some sports magazines. "I thought we were supposed to be . . . you know?"

"It's boring here," Eesha said, putting the magazine back on the rack. "Let's go."

Ike shook his head. This was all a waste of time. Maybe she'd just wanted to see if he would really come along.

"Yeah," he said. "Sure."

As they walked back out after Eesha paid at the register, something curious caught Ike's eye. It was a bumper sticker on a Ford F-150 truck parked near their bikes that read: *I Want to Believe.* Next to the words was a picture of a UFO.

"Look at that," he said, pointing.

Eesha followed his finger. "Hmm. I guess the army has some believers."

"And I'm one of them," a voice behind them said.

Ike and Eesha both spun around.

It was a man in civilian clothes, carrying a bag of groceries. "You an *X-Files* fan, too?" he asked.

He looked to be around thirty, Ike guessed, with short red hair and glasses.

"I remember that show," Eesha said.

Ike had a vague memory of *The X-Files*. His mom used to watch when he was little. She said it was too scary for him, though. He often had nightmares when he was a kid.

"Lots of . . . *aliens* in that show," Eesha said, looking directly at the man.

Ike almost closed his eyes in embarrassment. She was so obvious.

"Yeah," the man replied, sliding into the driver's seat. "Better watch out. Nevada's a UFO hot spot, you know."

He slammed the door shut.

Ike and Eesha turned to look at each other, then watched the truck drive down the street.

"Well," Eesha started. "That was weird."

"Yeah," Ike replied, still watching the truck's taillights. "It was."

Chapter Five

Ike didn't hear from Eesha the next day. Or the day after. He put her conspiracy theories out of his mind. Their exploration of the base had turned out to be nothing more than a little joy ride. He wondered if this was all just some sort of game. One time, when they lived—he couldn't even remember where—some of his new friends had roped him into something called snipe hunting. Ike went along with it, thinking there was some magical beast in the forest. But it was all a big joke. On him. They did it to every new kid that moved to the base.

Today, unfortunately, his mom had given him a chore. On a Sunday, no less. He was supposed to go through the boxes that had been sitting in the basement since they'd moved in and set aside anything he wanted to keep. What he *really* wanted to do was play *Shadow Goons*, but that wasn't going to happen.

As he headed down to the basement, he peered through the kitchen window. His mom and dad were sitting in lawn chairs out back, listening to corny '90s music. Sometimes, when they were feeling—Ike tried to remember the word—*nostalgic*, that was it, they'd try to get him to dance with them. It was terrible and embarrassing. *For them.*

He flipped on the light at the top of the stairs and made his way down. The place looked like a bomb had gone off. Boxes upon boxes full of old clothes, record albums, toys, and who knew what else. They still had a lot of stuff that needed to be unpacked. His dad was a bit of a hoarder.

Ike started opening boxes and rooting through them. Most of the stuff was old and should have been thrown out before they moved to Mercury: broken action figures he played with when he was little, dorky clothes he no longer wore, and lots of puzzles. They were his favorite hobby years ago, and he and his mom used to spend hours at the kitchen table sorting through the pieces.

He moved to another part of the basement, over by the area that housed the boiler and HVAC system. Cobwebs hung from the wooden rafters. He wasn't about to clean that up. *Nope*, he thought. *Not getting anywhere near spiders.*

He noticed their old footlocker pushed up against the far wall. Ike used to dig through it when he was on the hunt for hidden treasures. It was huge and painted standard military green with giant snap buckles. US ARMY was stamped in white stencil lettering on the top. He undid both latches and pushed the top back, releasing a squeaking groan.

The medicinal smell of mothballs rose up to greet him. He wrinkled his nose. It was a funny smell. What were mothballs made of, anyway? He remembered his grandmother had an old chest that smelled the same way. Looking at all of the things stuffed into the trunk brought back a flood of memories: old survival manuals, metal pots and pans that folded up for camping, a Swiss Army knife that he took out and put in his pocket, and one of his mother's old military uniforms. He even found his childhood stuffed animal, Hector the Protector, a giant dog with floppy ears. His mom had bought it for him when his tonsils were taken out when he was nine. "You did well, Hector," Ike said, closing the lid. "Good job."

Another box to his right drew his attention. It was marked with big bold letters: SW RADIO. Ike had never seen it before. He opened up the flaps and peered inside.

Hmm. What's this?

He pulled it out. It looked old, like something they used way back in the '90s. Dials and little meters were under a glass display. The front had lots of knobs marked with different letters and numbers: SW1, SW2, SW3. There were also other labels like Xtal Marker and Band Spread Dial.

The word Voice was above a little screen. *A microphone?*

Ike blew the dust from the cover, then sneezed as loud as a cannon burst.

He couldn't put his finger on why, but he felt as if he had just stumbled upon something very, very important.

☆ ☆ ☆

Upstairs in his room, he plugged the radio into the wall socket and set it on his desk. A small, dim light on the meters grew in brilliance until it was bright yellow. Static suddenly filled his ears. "Where's the volume?" he asked himself, alarmed.

The noise suddenly turned into a high-pitched squeal. Ike fumbled with the buttons and turned one of the little black knobs to the left. The screeching noise faded.

"Phew," he said aloud.

The little glass pane was yellow with age. Small red daggers jumped to attention as he turned the biggest knob to SW1. It was the tuner, he assumed. A voice in an unknown language wafted from the speaker. It was like something he'd once heard in school when they were studying different cultures. *Russian?* He continued to turn the dial. Now there was someone speaking in French. Now German.

He switched the dial to SW2.

Carnival music.

Ike had a sudden memory of when he was little, riding

on a carousel with gleaming-teeth horses. "Strange," he whispered.

But then a voice spoke in English, broken by bursts of static:

"3, 9, 2, 3, 1, 4, 0, 7, 14, 38, 12 . . . eyes only . . ."

Ike gasped and leaned in closer.

"Report Kilo. Report Kilo."

The voice and music vanished as suddenly as they had come, leaving only ghostly static coming from the speaker.

Ike sat frozen. His ears rang. *Eyes only? Kilo?*

What did it mean?

A tingle rose up his spine.

Whatever it was, it was certainly mysterious.

And there was nothing Ike liked more than solving a mystery.

Chapter Six

Ike kept the radio in his room and went back down to the basement to finish going through the boxes. He didn't find anything else of interest, but he made sure to straighten up the area and put the stuff that needed to be thrown out into a pile. That should satisfy his mom, he hoped.

He barely slept that night. The voice from the radio kept running through his head.

Eyes only. Report Kilo.

He wanted to tell Eesha.

But he wasn't sure.

Just because he'd come across an old radio and some mysterious words and numbers didn't mean it had anything to do with whatever their parents were doing here in Mercury, Nevada. But still, there was a chance that it meant *something*. And even if it had *nothing* to do with the base, it was still a pretty cool mystery.

He got out of bed and went downstairs just as his mom and dad were about to leave for work. He scratched his head and sat down. Reluctantly, he picked up the box of Great Grainy Goodness and poured the cereal into a bowl set out for him. "Eat up, son," his father told him. "Breakfast's the most important meal of the day."

"And it's sugar-free," his mom added.

"Great," Ike replied. "Gotta love sugar-free."

"We'll both be home late," his mom said, ignoring his snarky comment and grabbing her car keys from the table. "There's some leftover tofu lasagna in the fridge if you get hungry for lunch."

Ike's dad shot him a conspiratorial side-eye, and Ike returned it.

After they left, Ike ate his cereal slowly, still thinking about the message on the radio. He had to talk to Eesha. She seemed to know a lot about . . . unusual stuff.

He paused, mid-chew.

Were he and Eesha friends? He had to talk to someone about the voice, and he didn't want to ask his parents. On the off chance that the message *did* have something to do with his mom's work and the base, he didn't want them to know he was snooping around.

He took out his phone to text Eesha and realized he

didn't have her info. They'd forgotten to exchange numbers. That left him with only one option. He had to talk to her in person.

☆ ☆ ☆

He darted upstairs and brushed his teeth, then grabbed the radio. He wondered for a moment if he should put it in a box or a pillowcase or something, but decided against it and just carried it.

Outside, the sky was a brilliant blue. A military cargo plane—a C-5, Ike thought it was called—rumbled slowly overhead. His dad said they weighed over two hundred and eighty tons! Ike still wasn't sure how something that big got up into the air. *How do UFOs fly?* he wondered. One of the videos he'd watched said that they used some kind of antigravity mechanism, something that the military had tried to reverse engineer. Ike didn't really understand all of it, but it was fascinating.

He walked at a leisurely pace. The military was all about uniformity, and base housing was no exception. All of the homes were built close together, with nothing but a driveway and a front lawn between them. Most were painted white, but every now and then Ike came across a beige one. To be honest, he couldn't even tell you if his house was beige or white. That's how bland it all was. The lawns were perfectly trimmed, and the *tick-tick-tick* of sprinklers provided a soothing soundtrack. American flags waved from every home.

Eesha's house came into view. Ike paused. He was nervous. What would she think of him coming over? He stepped off the sidewalk and up to the Webbs' front door. A welcome mat proclaimed: *America, Love It or Leave It.*

He rang the bell.

Within seconds, the door flew open. Jack and Jill stared at him. They both wore sheets with a hole cut out for their heads. Why were they dressed for Halloween in June? "Boo!" he said, and they both shrieked and ran past him, like prisoners making a run for it. He watched as they fled down the sidewalk, almost tripping over their ghostly sheets. He turned back to the open door and cautiously stepped inside. "Eesha?" he called, not too loudly.

He didn't want her coming downstairs and mistaking him for a burglar. She'd probably tackle him to the ground and squeeze all the air out of him. He stepped a little farther into the living room right as Eesha came bounding down the stairs.

"Ike?" she said, alarmed. "What are you doing here? Where are the twins?"

Ike swallowed. "They answered the door and ran outside."

Eesha sprinted to the open door and leaned out half-way. "Jack!" she shouted. "Jill! Get back here!"

She turned back around to face him and shook her head in exasperation. "Little nerd-bots."

Ike chuckled.

There was a moment of silence. Ike stared at his sneakers. Fortunately, the awkwardness was broken by the return of Jack and Jill, looking defeated. "You're only supposed to play in the backyard," Eesha scolded them.

Both kids groaned loudly and headed toward the kitchen and then out the back door. Ike heard it slam shut.

Once they were gone, Eesha turned to stare at him again. "So, what are you doing here, anyway?"

And then, as if she had only just now noticed what he was holding, added, "What is that thing?"

"There's something I need to show you," Ike told her. "I was gonna text you, but I didn't have your number."

"Oh," Eesha said, and then fell silent.

Ike wondered what she was thinking.

With the twins in the safe confines of the backyard, Eesha led Ike down to their basement. For a family that had only just moved in, the space was in complete opposition to the mess in Ike's house. There was a bookshelf with neat rows of books, a fake fireplace with electric logs, an old couch, a beanbag, and a few chairs around a small table.

"So," Eesha said. "What is it?"

Ike set the radio down on the table.

"It's a radio of some sort. I found it in a box in our basement. I heard something strange on it and thought, well . . . I thought you might wanna check it out."

Eesha gave him a curious grin. She walked over to a little HVAC closet and came back out with an extension cord a moment later. "Here," she said. Ike took the cord and plugged it into the wall behind him and then into the radio. They both sat down opposite each other.

"That's pretty old-school," Eesha pointed out. "Never seen one like that before. Well, actually, I've hardly ever seen any."

Ike nodded and turned the power on. The little yellow light began to glow. Eesha leaned in. Ike hadn't changed the channel since the day before. He'd wanted to make sure he could find it again.

"Fascinating," Eesha said bluntly, as static filled the air.

Ike felt foolish. He'd really thought he was onto something. Maybe it was just a onetime thing. A joke.

But then . . .

The eerie carnival music piped through the speaker.

"3, 9, 2, 3, 1, 4, 0, 7, 14, 38, 12 . . . eyes only . . ."

"That's it!" Ike shouted, a little too loudly.

Eesha sat up straight in her chair. "What's it mean? 'Eyes only'?"

"No idea. Some kind of code, maybe?"

The voice faded.

"I think that's all," Ike said, deflated.

"Report Sierra," the voice came again. "Report Sierra."

"Oooh, this is wild!" Eesha exclaimed.

"I know, right?" Ike replied. "Wait a minute. Yesterday it said, 'report Kilo.'"

"'Kilo'?"

"Yeah. It read the numbers and then said 'eyes only' and 'report Kilo.'"

"Who's Kilo?"

"I don't know. Who or what is Sierra?"

They stood staring at the radio in silence.

"Hmm," Eesha murmured. "We need to look this up."

"Look what up?"

Eesha smirked. "You know, on the internet? Do a search for old radio, numbers, music, voices."

Ike slapped his forehead, just like a cartoon character. He hadn't even thought of that.

"Be right back," Eesha said, and clomped up the stairs. Ike stared around the room. Could they really be onto something? Something really . . . secret? He was excited by the prospect of it, whether it had anything to do with the base or not.

A moment later Eesha came racing back with her laptop. She sat down across from him again and flipped it open.

"Search for radio, numbers, and music," Ike put in.

"Duh," she moaned. "I already said that."

Ike shrunk.

Eesha typed a lot faster than Ike, which he was surprised by, for some reason. He thought since she was into sports, she wouldn't be that good at typing. Which didn't make sense, he realized. *Don't make assumptions about people*, his parents had often told him.

"This has to be it," Eesha said.

"What?" Ike asked, getting up to peer over her shoulder. The screen showed images of old radios and a bunch of text and numbers on little sheets of white paper.

"They're called numbers stations," she went on, "and they were used on short-wave radios like this one during . . . the Cold War!"

"Cold War?" Ike whispered.

"Yeah," Eesha replied. "The Cold War was when Russia and the US—"

"I know what the Cold War was," Ike said flatly.

Eesha ignored him. "It says that these numbers stations

were used to send messages to spies in the field. The numbers were usually locations or directions. Look. They have some videos."

Ike and Eesha watched various videos for the next hour, pausing once to check on the twins. Most of the videos started with odd music, which they learned was a signal that the code was about to start. Some of the stations were pretty famous, and lots of people studied them as a hobby. One of the oldest stations was called UVB-76, also known as "The Buzzer," which had been running nonstop since the late '70s. It was a constant one-note buzz on the band 4625 kHz. No government had ever acknowledged the existence of numbers stations, even though the signals had come from the United States, Russia, and all over the globe.

"Incredible," Ike said. "What do we do now?"

Eesha continued to scroll through the search results. "Fascinating. The only way they can be deciphered is with something called a onetime pad. Look."

Ike leaned in. The photo showed a piece of paper with columns of random letters and numbers filling the whole page.

"How do you decipher *that*?" he asked. "Looks like you'd have to be a math genius."

"It says you can only use it once and then it's no good,"

Eesha said. "It's like a key of some sort."

"So cool," Ike put in.

"It's all so . . . low-tech," Eesha said. "Doesn't leave any digital footprints."

"So," Ike said. "If we can find the . . . onetime pad, we might be able to decipher it!"

"Right. And you said you found this radio in your basement?"

"Yeah. It was packed away in a box next to our old footlocker. Never seen it before."

Eesha nodded. Ike could practically see the gears in her mind turning. She chewed her fingernails for a moment. "If this is a message that needs to be deciphered, that must mean your mom or dad has to have another radio, too, right? How else would they hear the message, if this one was boxed up in the basement?"

Eesha had a point, but Ike wasn't sure the message was meant for his parents. Actually, the whole thing was pretty ridiculous, he realized, but Eesha and her enthusiasm had a way of pulling him into her orbit.

"*And*," she went on, "if they have a way of hearing the message, they must have the onetime pad."

Ike fell silent. The awkwardness was suddenly gone. Whatever they were trying to figure out was serious.

Eesha pushed herself away from the table and stood up. She stared at him for a long moment.

"Ike, I think you need to snoop around your parents' room."

Chapter Seven

They met up several times over the next week, alternating between houses. Their parents were thrilled, thinking that they were becoming fast friends again. Ike had to admit, they kind of *were* friends—but only because they were trying to figure out what was going on at Mercury Army Base. But he couldn't get up the courage to search his parents' room, much to Eesha's annoyance.

"I searched *my* parents' room," she'd said. "I even tried to go through their emails. And their jobs aren't even suspicious! I told you they always work the same jobs wherever we go."

Good for her, Ike thought. *But I can't search my parents' room. It's not right.* Plus, who knew what he might find that he *didn't* want to know about?

His mom and dad went about their daily routines, and Ike saw nothing suspicious. He often thought he was being silly for even suspecting them.

In the meantime, the Fourth of July was coming up,

and a big celebration was planned complete with fireworks and a band. Most importantly, it was happening on the base. It would be a perfect time to try to snoop around a bit.

☆ ☆ ☆

July fourth arrived hot and sunny. Ike was trying to decide what T-shirt to wear: *Black Nerds Unite* or *Zombie Killer*. In the end, he decided on a plain black one.

"Ike," his mom moaned when she saw him. "That black shirt is going to soak up the heat like a sponge! Why don't you put on that nice white shirt I bought you?"

"I like this one," he complained.

"Okay," she said, shaking her head. "If you want to burn up in this Nevada heat, be my guest."

Whatever, Ike thought, but he didn't dare say it out loud.

On the way to the celebration, he pressed his nose up against the car window. American flags were everywhere: snapping in the breeze on flagpoles and planted on little sticks in front yards. A kid on a bicycle rolled by on the sidewalk, a flag waving behind him. Military bases were the most patriotic places on Earth, he realized.

He saw the crowds before they reached their destination. The event was to be held on one of the large expanses of green lawn that served as a training ground for new recruits. Ike assumed it was some kind of artificial turf. Any other time he would have seen several units of young men and women being put through the ringer as they exercised in the blazing sun, all the while being shouted at by drill instructors with buzz cuts. But today, it was different. Big tents and tables were set up everywhere. His dad parked the car in an almost full lot, and they got out. The first thing Ike smelled was sizzling hamburgers. His stomach rumbled.

Once they all climbed out of the car, Ike took a look around. He saw several people who were definitely not military. He could tell by their clothes, their hair, their overall . . . *vibe*. They must have gotten background checks by the MPs before being allowed through the gates. Most of the people who lived in the small town outside the base worked at fast-food restaurants, malls, and gas stations. There just wasn't much industry or commerce nearby.

Giant speakers blasted patriotic music, all loud brass and the *rat-a-tat-tat* of rapid drumming. Little kids chased each other, screaming the whole while. Red-white-and-blue tablecloths covered the picnic tables. Two lemonade stands run by teenagers already had long lines. There was even a face-painting station. Dogs were everywhere, making acrobatic leaps to catch Frisbees.

"What's up, weirdo?"

Ike spun around.

Eesha punched him on the shoulder.

"Ouch!" he yelped, rubbing the spot. "Do you have to do that?"

She laughed. "Weakling."

"Doofus," he said, pushing his glasses back up on the bridge of his nose.

A sudden crash of cymbals drew their attention, but nothing happened afterward so they went on with their conversation.

"Uh," he started. "Find out anything more about those . . . pad cipher things?"

"Onetime pads," Eesha corrected him. "I searched my parents' room again but came up empty." She stared at him. "What about you?"

Ike bit his lip. What if his mom had a onetime pad hidden away somewhere so she could figure out the code? *Impossible*, he thought. It was pretty far-fetched to think that the radio message was intended for her. It was probably for some colonel or spy somewhere. If it even *was* a real message. More likely, it was just kids fooling around. Just like him and Eesha, he realized.

"No," he said.

Eesha frowned in disappointment.

"Uh," Ike started. "Want to explore a little?"

"Sure."

They surveyed the area while their parents and the twins spread out on blankets. Nothing seemed out of the ordinary. Ike peered at the nondescript gray and beige buildings that surrounded them. Most of them were marked with a giant single letter painted black: A, E, S, and others. There didn't seem to be any rhyme or reason to it. He and Eesha wanted to get closer, but every one of the buildings had guards stationed around them.

Ike spied his mom and dad watching him and Eesha. His parents smiled and waved happily, obviously pleased to see them together. They both hesitantly waved back, then looked at each other and rolled their eyes.

With nothing new to conspire about, they spent a little time wandering around, eating burgers and hot dogs. Eesha said she could make an exception to her "training" and gobbled down two hot dogs and a funnel cake. She also had her face painted, but Ike wasn't interested. Plus, he had sensitive skin and didn't want to break out in a rash or something. He could imagine Eesha teasing him for his sudden outbreak of hives. *Dude. Your face is like zit city.*

The sun was slowly setting, and people were getting ready for the main event: fireworks. Ike took a spot on the blanket his parents had brought, and Eesha sat with her family. He was looking forward to the explosions of color and the way his whole body vibrated to the sound of the thunderous booms.

At last, it was dark out. The stars were bright, seeing as how they were in a small town without a lot of light pollution. There were no skyscrapers in Mercury. A loudspeaker crackled, and as the music ended, a voice drifted out over the crowd. Ike had no idea who the speaker was, but he was clean-cut and dressed in "civvies," which is what military people called their ordinary clothes.

"Ladies and gentlemen, friends and family. Today we celebrate the independence of our great nation. From the amber fields of grain to the purple mountain majesties."

Ike always thought it was "purple *mountain's* majesties." He'd have to look it up.

The voice went on, but something drew his attention away. Near the stage, where the speaker stood in front of a screen with an image of the Washington Monument, a group of men and women huddled close together. Every now and then, one of them held their hand up to their ear as if listening to a Bluetooth device.

They wore a uniform Ike had never seen before. Black jackets, white dress shirts, and dark blue pants with a gold stripe running down the leg. Several diagonal stripes were on their left sleeves. There were badges and medals on their uniforms too, but Ike couldn't make all of them out. There seemed to be some disagreement among them, and one man in particular was very agitated. He paced and spoke into his shoulder, like some kind of Secret Service guy.

Suddenly, one of the women walked onto the stage. The speaker turned quickly, caught off guard. He backed away from the microphone and nodded along as she whispered something in his ear, then immediately left the stage, leaving the host looking very perplexed. He ran his hand through his hair and leaned into the microphone. "Um," he began, over squeaking feedback. "I'm afraid we have some unfortunate news. The fireworks show has been canceled."

A chorus of moans rippled through the audience.

"I'm sorry, folks. There seems to be some sort of safety issue. But, please, don't let it dampen our patriotic spirit! There's still plenty of food to go around. We have . . . um, a dessert truck with apple pie and ice cream right now. So . . . God bless America!" He finished by pumping his fist in the air.

A weak smattering of applause went up. Ike watched as the mysterious figures got into a black SUV and departed, taillights blurring in the distance.

Ike caught Eesha's eye, sitting with her family a few feet away. Her eyebrows were raised in question, just like his.

As the music started up again, he made his way over to her. She got up as he approached. The twins were eating ice cream cones, half of which was already on their shirts. Ike gave her a conspiratorial nod, and they headed away from their families and toward the stage, where a few people were still gathered.

"Did you see that?" he asked.

"Yup," Eesha confirmed, looking around. "That was really bizarre. Why in the world would they stop the fireworks display? And who were those . . . other guys? The ones in uniform?"

"Don't know," Ike muttered. "But one of them had on a badge I recognized."

Ike recalled a memory from when he was little. He loved military badges and medals, and was proud to have a collection. There was one that he'd really wanted, but his mom said she couldn't get it for him. But he did remember the design: a key, a torch, and a lightning bolt.

"It was an INSCOM badge," he said.

"'Inscom'? What's that?"

"It stands for United States Army Intelligence and Security Command."

Eesha paused. "Sounds serious. Do you know what they're all about?"

Ike searched his memories. "I don't know if I remember . . ."

Eesha whipped out her phone.

"Oh," Ike said. "*Duh.* Good idea."

Eesha tapped away for a moment. "LOL. It's all written in that military lingo."

Ike knew exactly what she was talking about. The military vocabulary was a language all its own. His dad once used the word *discombobulated* instead of *messy.* He was talking about Ike's room, of course.

"What's it say?"

"'Mission command of operational intelligence . . . works in partnership with the National Security Agency.' Let's see, what else . . ."

Her face froze.

"What?" Ike drew closer, and they stood side by side. He peered over her shoulder.

Eesha drew a breath. "Most of their missions are classified. 'Once used . . . *paranormal* research for . . . remote viewing, which is a psychic technique to see things over a great distance without physically being there.'"

Ike's head spun. "This is—that's nuts!"

"There's more," Eesha said. "Get ready to flip out."

Ike swallowed.

Eesha looked back to her phone. "'Has been known to operate in the field of . . . *cryptography* for secure communications.'"

"Holy . . ." Ike started.

Eesha looked up from her phone. "Ike?"

"Yeah?"

"There's definitely something weird going on around here."

Ike had to agree. Things were getting very strange in Mercury, Nevada.

Chapter Eight

Ike plucked a blank notebook from his shelf and wrote TOP SECRET in black marker on the front. Pretty obvious, he realized. But still, he had to keep a record of what they were discovering. And the government could hack phones and computers, so he didn't want to take any chances. He and Eesha had to figure out the numbers from the radio station and how it was all connected. Find that onetime pad, the code key.

He'd asked his mom about the military people that stopped the celebration but she only shrugged and said she didn't know. Ike wasn't sure he bought it.

Who were those people? What were they doing there? Why would they stop the celebration? Remote viewing? Cryptography? Did his parents know about this branch of the military?

He made his way down the stairs. No one was in the kitchen. *Good*, he thought. *Maybe I can find something to eat that doesn't taste like bird food.*

He opened the refrigerator. Perhaps his dad had hidden some bacon in there somewhere. He pulled out the bins, but there was no bacon to be found, only a few dried apples, a couple of oranges, a loaf of bread, and a bunch of other healthy stuff. He grabbed an apple and sat down. A sheet of paper was on the table in front of him. He picked it up.

Honey, thought I'd let you sleep in.
Had to get to the base early.
Find something to eat. See you tonight,
Love, Mom

Ike set the note back down. She was always going in early these days. Did it mean something unusual was happening? He shook the thought away. His imagination was getting the best of him, thanks to Eesha.

But, his inner voice taunted him, *what about the numbers station? And those INSCOM people? That wasn't normal, right?*

He took a bite of the apple and then screwed up his face. It tasted bad. The skin was soft and wrinkly. He got up and spit the mushy mouthful into the trash and then tossed the apple in after. His mom would freak if she saw him spit in the trash can. But where else was he supposed to put it?

Upstairs, he brushed his teeth and threw on some shorts. He didn't really like wearing shorts, but it had been so hot lately, he didn't care. He took his mom's advice and put on a white shirt, a barrier against the sun.

As he passed his parents' bedroom, he paused. Eesha said she had searched *her* parents' room.

No, Ike told himself. His mom and dad always told him to respect people's boundaries and privacy.

But what if something's in there? It'll only take a minute. Don't snoop, just take a look around.

Ike exhaled a worried breath.

"Forgive me, Mom," he said. "Dad."

And then he stepped into their room.

The bed was tidy and neat. Even the sheets were gathered tight at the corners, not even showing the slightest wrinkle. Ike could never get that right, no matter how many times his dad had shown him. He said the sheet should be so tight you could bounce a quarter on it.

Ike peered around the room. It was one big tribute to the military. His mom's medals were framed under glass and hung on the wall, along with several official-looking letters that proclaimed her "distinguished career."

An exercise bike sat in the corner, his dad's sweatpants draped over the bars. Ike knew his dad wanted to turn the basement into a home gym one day. *Good*, he'd thought when his dad told him. *I'll be sure to stay away.*

He scanned the bedside tables. Books on military topics, biographies of great generals and men and women of service, his mom's word-search puzzles. He picked one up from the stack and flipped through it. His mom loved going through them and solving all of the challenges. She did them every morning.

He stared at the thin, newsprint page in front of him, rows and rows of jumbled letters. He turned to a page with a yellow sticky on it. The puzzle had yet to be solved, but above several of the letters was a check mark.

"Hmm," he murmured.

Maybe she had just been doodling, he tried to reason. But another thought crept to the front of his brain.

No. It can't be.

He stood there. Frozen.

Did he just find the code? The onetime pad? Maybe these check-marked letters spelled out some kind of word or message when they were unscrambled.

Ike's palms grew clammy. His heart raced.

Breathe, he told himself. *Breathe.*

He smoothed the open pages with his hands and set it

on the bed, then took out his phone. *Here goes*, he thought.

Click. Click. Click.

After taking several pictures, he carefully placed the book back on the bedside table, just the way he'd found it.

You've done it now, a voice in his head accused him.

No turning back.

Chapter Nine

His worry only grew as he made his way to Eesha's. He may have just done something very illegal. Stealing state secrets or something. Then again, he and Eesha were probably just letting their imaginations get the better of them. She was the one who started all of this in the first place. Maybe she was suffering from some sort of delusion and had pulled him into her imaginary world, too.

UFOs? Aliens? Secret codes? *Really?*

If his mom *was* involved in something mysterious, what would he do? Was she really "keeping the nation safe," as she had said?

Ike was standing in front of Eesha's door before he knew it, his mind still racing. She let him in and led him down to the basement. "What's going on?" she'd asked, but Ike refused to answer until they were safe from prying ears. The twins were planted upstairs in front of a TV with the volume turned all the way up.

They both sat on the couch. Eesha was staring at him. He wondered if he was doing the right thing. He took out his phone. "I found something." He scrolled through his photos and showed her the pictures he'd taken.

"Word search?" she said. "Really?"

"My mom always does these. Every morning. She's worked on them for as long as I can remember. What if this is like the onetime pad?"

Eesha tilted her head. "Can I see it?" she asked, holding out her hand. Ike gave her his phone. She used her thumb and forefinger to zoom in on the pictures. "Hmm."

"What?"

"Check marks above some of these letters."

"I know, right?"

Eesha nodded to herself, thinking. "Okay. First things first." She stood up, walked to the table, and sat down. Ike followed and took a seat opposite her. Eesha set the phone on the table and rubbed her hands together in anticipation. "Process of elimination. Let's write down the letters that have checks and see if they form a message."

"That's what I was thinking," Ike put in. "I wanted to come over so we could work on it . . . together."

Eesha actually smiled. Not sarcastically but an actual, genuine smile.

Ike dug around in his backpack and pulled out his Top

Secret notebook. Eesha got up and plucked a pen from an old coffee mug on the bookshelf. For the next half hour they tried every combination they could think of, with no luck. The checked letters didn't spell out anything at all, just a few random words that didn't seem to have any connection.

Eesha paused, seemingly lost in thought. Then she snapped her fingers. "The numbers! From the radio. Did you write them down?"

Ike flipped through his notebook. "Here they are," he said, turning to the page.

Eesha studied the numbers intently. "Maybe, just maybe . . ."

"What?" Ike asked, tired of her cryptic clues.

"Look," she said. "There are . . . ten rows of letters going across, right?"

"Right," he replied, looking at the photo of the word-search book.

"And," she went on, "there are ten rows going down."

Ike cocked his head. "Ah. I see. If we think of the first letter as number one, and the second letter as two, each letter has a numerical value."

"Right." Eesha smiled slyly. "You're finally catching on."

Ike grinned.

"Give me a blank page," she demanded. "And read me the numbers from the radio. The first number was three, I think, right?"

"Yup. The first number's three."

"Great," she replied. She raised the pencil to her lips and dabbed it against her tongue.

People do that with pens, Ike thought. *Not pencils.* She must have seen it in a movie and thought it looked cool.

"Read 'em off," Eesha said.

Ike took a breath, and then began to read: "3, 9, 2, 3, 1 . . ."

Eesha wrote carefully, enlarging the photo on Ike's phone so she could see the letters clearly and count the rows. Ike noticed that she was left-handed. When he was a kid, he'd wanted to be left-handed, but his right won out.

He fidgeted as they worked. He was getting even more nervous. What if they found out that his mom was doing something top secret? What would they do then?

Eesha raised her head. She stared at the page. "Hmpf. Doesn't make any sense."

"Let me see," Ike said.

She turned the paper around. Ike studied it and then spoke the letters aloud: "T-X-L-F-N-V-L-O-Y-H-U." He looked at Eesha. "And this is what comes out when you match up the radio numbers to the rows of letters?"

"Yup," she said, sitting back. "Make any sense to you?"

Ike shook his head. "Nope."

They both tried to figure it out, rearranging the letters, trying to make more than one word, but in the end, they came up empty.

They sat in silence a moment, but for the blaring TV upstairs.

"Maybe it's another language?" Eesha ventured.

Ike's eyes lit up. "My mom does speak a little German. She was deployed at Ramstein Air Base in Germany before I was born."

"Do you?" Eesha asked. "Speak German?"

Ike shook his head. *"Nein."*

Eesha smirked. "If it was secret, don't you think they would've used something more difficult than a word-search book?"

A wave of embarrassment rose up Ike's neck.

"Nice try, though," Eesha consoled him.

Ike felt like an idiot. She must have picked up on it.

"Should we try to do some research on INSCOM?" she asked. "Or check out the radio again?"

But Ike had already made up his mind. They were acting like kids. There was no secret message. All of this was just a bunch of nonsense.

"Nah," he said, standing up. "I'm gonna go."

Eesha made a sour face, and then chewed a fingernail. "Okay, fine," she said coldly.

And then, without another word, she led him upstairs and showed him to the door.

Chapter Ten

Ike walked home feeling foolish. Not only had he gotten wrapped up in Eesha's dumb conspiracy theories, but he had done something worse:

Invaded his parents' privacy.

That was unforgivable.

Sure, the discovery of the short-wave radio and numbers stations was interesting, but that was about it. There was absolutely nothing pointing to his mom or dad being involved in some kind of shadowy, top secret government project.

What about the officers at the Fourth of July celebration?

He didn't know who they were or why they had canceled the fireworks show, but it probably wasn't anything . . . he searched for the right word . . . *nefarious.*

He actually chuckled as he walked. "What a doofus," he said aloud as he made his way home. "Ike, you're a goofball."

☆ ☆ ☆

Ike jumped back into *Shadow Goons*. He hadn't played in a while and was itching for a zombie fight. *I need to get on with the important stuff,* he told himself, *like playing games and going exploring.*

Over the next several days, he did exactly that, even venturing out a little farther than on his previous expeditions. During this whole escapade with Eesha, he'd wanted to believe there was something strange going on, but now he realized it was just the wild imagination of two kids, looking for mysteries.

He still watched his mom carefully, as if she might accidentally reveal something, but nothing ever came to light. She was just a military mom doing her job. *Keeping the nation safe,* just like she'd said.

Ike spent a *lot* more time on *Shadow Goons*. He made it to level thirty and was rewarded with a legendary weapon called the Sword of the Sun, which could knock out zombie hordes with one swing. He also started a fantasy story about a kid on a military base who discovered he was a long-lost ancestor of King Arthur.

He and Eesha hadn't texted in days. He guessed they weren't really friends after all. *Mom was right,* he told himself. *Little Mr. Play-Alone. You always wanted to be by yourself.*

And that was exactly what he was going to do. Maybe he'd make some friends at school when summer break was over.

He hadn't been exploring as much as he had hoped. It was just too hot. But today, he really felt the need to feel the sun on his skin.

It was scorching outside, as usual, but he'd brought his canteen of water. After a half hour of walking, it was almost gone, even though he'd promised himself he'd try to conserve it. He took his time as he walked, taking pictures of interesting shrubs and rocks. He thought that the slower he walked, the less he would sweat, but that was proven wrong very quickly.

As he made his way through an unfamiliar part of the woods, he found a giant cement mixer lying on the forest floor, like the bones of an old dinosaur. A discarded metal sign on the ground proclaimed: NO TRESPASSING. It was rusty and weather-stained, and looked like it had been in the sun for a hundred years. *Doesn't mean anything anymore*, Ike told himself, and went to investigate.

As he drew closer, he saw that the cement mixer was just the big barrel part, the drum, that spun around as the gravel was mixed, or however it was made. There was no danger of being trapped inside because both ends were big circular openings. He took a picture of it for *Ike's Journal of*

Amazing and Fascinating Things.

He stepped inside and immediately felt relief from the hot sun. The bottom was littered with old bottles and newspapers. It smelled a little musty, too. He hoped that no animals had gone to the bathroom in it.

He pushed some of the newspapers away with his foot and lowered himself to sit against the wall. His parents probably wouldn't approve of him hanging around in here. He was pretty far from home, for one, and he was sure his dad would say that abandoned machinery was dangerous. But there wasn't any working machinery anywhere near it, he told himself. *I'm not bothering anybody.*

He raised his canteen to his lips and took another drink, savoring every drop. He shook the canteen. *Not a lot left.*

He thought about the rabbit hole he and Eesha had gone down. *Dork*, he scolded himself. He reached into his bag, took out his notebook, and began to work on his novel. It still needed a title. He flipped back to find the first page of the story and saw the numbers from the radio station. *What do these words and numbers really mean?* he asked himself against his better judgment. *Eyes only. Report Kilo. Report Sierra.*

He didn't want to get all wound up again, but he

couldn't help his curiosity. *Eyes only* must have meant the message was intended for only one person. *Report Kilo—* no idea. And what about the numbers?

He let out a breath. He hadn't touched the radio in days. When he got back home, he'd listen again to see if anything had changed. *And,* he promised himself, *that would be the last of it.*

He gathered up his belongings and stepped out of the cement mixer. He glanced at the old rusty warning sign again, but something else caught his eye.

Footprints.

In a mound of soft dirt.

Ike knelt down to take a closer look. At first, he thought they must belong to a dog or some other domesticated animal, but it couldn't be. This creature, whatever it was, had four long toes, with a point at the very end of each, like a claw of some sort. *A lizard?* He was in the desert after all, and geckos and iguanas were everywhere. But this was too big.

No.

This was something heavy. Something that weighed a lot. He could tell by the impression the footprint had left in the soil. It was deep. He thought of a documentary he'd watched about Bigfoot, and how an explorer had found strange footprints in the woods and made a plaster cast of them for further research. Ike had no idea how to do that. Instead, he took out his phone and snapped several pictures.

He rose back up and dusted off his jeans.

And that's when he saw more tracks.

They were a few feet away from where he stood, farther away than the ones he had just looked at. There was a trail of them, leading into the woods.

He drew in a breath. The forest had suddenly gone very still. He didn't even hear any birds.

Slowly, he followed the tracks. They were spaced far apart, as if whatever had made them was *huge*. The distance between them was bigger than a kid's footprints. *A man? Some kind of creature?*

He stepped carefully, following the tracks farther into the forest until fallen leaves and broken branches obscured the trail. He stayed still for several moments, listening. Nothing. Finally, he turned back around.

Hissss.

Ike froze, his breath in his throat.

He spun around to the snapping of branches and the sound of quick footfalls. Something was moving through the forest, retreating back to wherever it had come from. Ike swallowed his fear. Nervous energy flowed through his body.

Slowly, he turned back around. He heard his heartbeat in his ears. He started to walk, one careful step at a time. Whatever it was could be looking at him this very moment.

He didn't take a breath until he was back at his front door.

☆ ☆ ☆

Ike drank the last few drops of water in his canteen just before he reached home. When he got there, the first thing he did was to push a glass up against the cold-water dispenser on the fridge. He threw his head back and took several giant gulps.

"Somebody's thirsty," his mom said.

"Mom? What are you doing home?"

"Just decided to take a little break."

A break from what? Ike mused. *Top secret military projects? Does she know what "eyes only" and "report Kilo" mean?*

She walked over to stand at the sink, then looked out the window. Ike heard her sigh.

"Mom?" he asked. "What's wrong?"

Natalie Pressure turned to look at him. She quickly went back to her no-nonsense, stiff-upper-lip military demeanor. "Nothing, honey. Just lots going on at work."

Like spy codes?

For a split second, he thought of telling her about Eesha's conspiracy theories and how he had been dragged into them, but thought better of it at the last minute. "Oh," he said instead. "Well, um, I hope you feel better."

"Thanks, Chipmunk," she replied.

Ike smiled at his old nickname. "Okay," he said. "I'm gonna go upstairs and take a bath. Went for a long expedition today."

"Oh, really?" his mom inquired. "Anything interesting?"

Just strange footprints and a monster's hiss. That's all.

"No. Not really."

"And how's Eesha?"

He bit his lip. "Okay, I guess. We haven't been hanging out the past few days."

His mother looked as if he had just told her he was dropping out of school to join the circus. "What? What happened?"

"Nothing. You know . . . we don't really have a lot in common, anyway."

She looked crestfallen. Her brow wrinkled. "And here I was thinking you two kids were best buds."

Ike didn't know what to say. His mother was looking at him in that concerned way parents do, like they're just waiting for you to tell them more. But he didn't.

Upstairs, after taking a long bath and putting on clean clothes, Ike looked up animal footprints on the internet but found nothing that resembled the tracks he'd seen, other than a lizard's. What could create such a strange—and *huge*—footprint?

He reached under the bed and took out the radio. He brought it over to his desk, plugged it into the wall, and turned it on. A low hum flowed from the speaker and then a blast of static. Each time he'd heard the numbers, it had been early morning or afternoon. It was later now, he realized. Maybe it only came on during certain hours.

The static suddenly went out.

The carousel music whirled up. Ike hadn't noticed it before, but it actually sounded like an old vinyl record. His dad had played one for him once, and the scratchy tone sounded exactly the same.

He leaned in a little closer. He didn't want to turn it up

too loud with his mom downstairs. He grabbed his note-book from the desk.

Footsteps sounded in the hallway. Ike shut off the radio and wheeled around in his chair.

His mom stood in the doorway.

"What are you doing with that radio?"

Chapter Eleven

Ike gulped and spun back around. "Oh," he started. "I found it down in the basement. Remember? You told me to clean out boxes down there?"

"Right," his mom said warily. "I did say that, didn't I?" *She's being weird.*

"I thought I'd just check it out," he said in as casual a way as he could muster.

His mom stepped farther into the room. Ike closed his notebook. His nerves were rattled.

Natalie Pressure's eyes roamed over her son's room. She seemed to take in every object: his rock collection, his bookshelf, the microscope on his desk, the small telescope by his bedside, until she finally landed back on the radio. "Thought I threw that old thing away. Hear anything interesting?"

Now Ike was really nervous. Was this just an innocent mom question or something deeper?

"Uh, no," he said. "Can't pick anything up. Just some old music and stuff."

She looked around once more. Ike felt as if she was searching for something.

"Okay, kiddo. Dinner's gonna be late. Dad's working overtime."

"Sure," Ike said softly.

His mom gave him one last curious look and then left, quietly closing the door behind her.

Ike rolled his chair back in front of his desk.

He released a bottled-up breath. Doubt and uncertainty flooded his mind. His mom sure did seem suspicious.

He had a decision to make. Too much was happening too fast. The weird footprints. That hissing sound. He had to tell Eesha. He just had to. Considering how their last conversation ended, he wasn't eager to talk to her. But he did.

He texted her the next morning:

Hey, it's me Ike

What do u want?

Need to talk to you about some stuff

What?

Ike pushed his glasses back up on his nose, worried. Here he was, getting sucked back into the whole thing.

He texted Eesha the directions to the cement mixer, and they agreed to meet there at noon. He didn't want to rush out and make his mom even more suspicious.

After eating breakfast, he headed back upstairs and passed the time listening to other numbers stations. The Buzzer was really mysterious. It was the one that had been transmitting a constant signal since the '70s, Eesha had said. Ike listened to the monotonous buzz for twenty minutes. He didn't know what he had expected to hear, but it was fascinating. Every now and then it was interrupted by a man's heavily accented, Russian-sounding voice: "Nikolai, Eva, Julia, Mikhail . . ."

He also found some other famous numbers stations called "The English Lady," "The Lincolnshire Poacher," and "Cherry Ripe," all with their own cryptic messages and numbers. Ike wondered what it all really meant. He was about to stash the radio back under the bed when he noticed a little plate on the bottom. The panel slid open to reveal four corroded D batteries. The large ones. He scraped away some of the powdery orange rust with a fingernail, but suddenly realized it wasn't a very good idea. Who knew what that stuff could do to your skin? He grabbed some Q-tips and rubbing alcohol from the bathroom and spent a few minutes cleaning the metal contacts.

Downstairs, he found some new batteries in a kitchen drawer and popped them in the radio, then rummaged in the closet for a shopping bag to carry it in. He didn't really know why he was taking it along, but now that it had batteries, he wouldn't need to plug it in. Maybe he and Eesha could listen again to see if anything had changed.

On the hike there, Ike thought about everything that had happened so far. He wavered back and forth between curiosity and doubt, but there was one thing he knew for certain: *something* odd was happening. He just wasn't sure what.

He got to the cement mixer first and looked for the tracks he'd seen before, kneeling a bit and searching the ground.

His heart fell.

They were no longer there.

They'd been disturbed.

He peered into the surrounding forest. What was the hissing sound he'd heard before? An animal? What kind of animal hisses? A snake? It was too loud to be a snake.

He walked to the cement mixer and settled inside, leaning back against the curved interior.

He sat in silence for a while and then turned on the radio. Classical music piped from the speaker. Ike leaned his head back and closed his eyes. The sound of flutes, timpani, and strings danced in his ears. He felt like he was being transported to another time and place, drifting away . . .

Footsteps crunched on fallen leaves.

Voices.

Kids' voices.

Ike shook himself awake and made his way out of the mixer.

Eesha was approaching. Ike was nervous and wondered how their meeting would go. After all, they did have a little argument the last time they were together. Well, he reflected, it wasn't *really* an argument. It was more like a shared frustration that ended up with him leaving her house.

Ike blinked. Eesha wore one of those safari hats and a pair of sunglasses, like it would really work as a disguise. But the thing that really got his attention was the twins. Jack and Jill were skipping happily alongside her, dressed as some sort of superheroes. The costumes looked home-made, with lots of aluminum foil and reflective safety tape. They both wore bicycle helmets painted bright red and, oddest of all, furry slippers. Ike stared, dumbfounded.

"I had to bring them," Eesha grumbled.

Ike was actually glad she'd brought the twins along. It helped break the tension. He laughed aloud at their costumes.

"What?" Eesha said, defensive. "I can't leave them at home! I'd be grounded."

"No worries," Ike said, almost laughing again.

Eesha turned to her sister and brother. She leaned down, placing her hands on her knees. "Me and Ike are gonna hang out, okay? You guys stay where I can see you." She rose back up, towering over them. "Or *else*."

The twins seemed to understand her threatening tone and were soon busy trying to build a fort out of fallen branches and rocks.

"Listen," Ike said. "When I was here the other day, I saw something really strange."

"Uh-huh," Eesha said doubtfully. "Like what?"

Her tone was already dismissive. Maybe she was still angry from the other day. "Tracks," he said.

"Tracks? What kind of tracks?"

Ike swallowed and dipped his head a moment before raising it back up.

"Well, they're gone now."

"Gone?"

"Yeah. They were right here. Where we're standing now." He paused. "But that's not the strangest part."

Eesha tilted her head.

"There was a hissing sound. Like . . . like some kind of . . . creature."

Eesha drew in a breath and looked to the ground and then back to the forest. "That is weird," she whispered.

"I know," Ike replied.

They climbed inside the cement mixer, with the kids still in view. Eesha took off her sunglasses and peered around. Her head almost brushed the top. "Awesome! How'd you find this place?"

"Just stumbled on it when I was exploring."

"Great." Eesha stared at him. "So, you're back on board?"

Ike hesitated for a moment. He swallowed. "I, uh . . . guess so."

"Cool!" she cheered.

Ike was relieved that their little spat was over.

"This is a good meeting place," Eesha went on. "What's

a secret project without a clandestine location?" She smiled mischievously.

"Clandestine," Ike repeated. "Good word choice."

Eesha folded her long legs to sit down next to him. "So, what's up? What'd you find out?"

"My mom came in my room and caught me with the radio. She looked . . . suspicious."

"Suspicious?"

"Yeah. She was asking me if I'd heard anything interesting, and she was looking around my room like she was searching for something. Plus, she said that work had been stressing her out lately."

Ike wondered if he was doing the right thing. This could all just send them down another conspiracy rabbit hole.

Eesha nodded, her face grave, as if he had just told her a nuclear missile was on its way to the army base. "Interesting. Very interesting."

They sat quietly for a moment. The twins were singing a song about dinosaurs.

"Why do you think that fireworks show was canceled?" Eesha asked.

"Don't know," Ike replied.

"Let's try to list the reasons. I'll start." She paused for

a moment, thinking. "Okay. It wasn't about the weather. It was clear and calm that night, right?"

Ike nodded. "Right. Maybe . . . maybe there were planes in the sky, and the fireworks would have gotten in the way of their flight paths or something."

"That's a pretty good theory."

"Or maybe," Ike went on, "maybe it has something to do with the sound? Like, not wanting to disturb something?"

"Like what?"

Ike shifted his back against the wall. "No idea."

"Hmm," Eesha murmured. She eyed the radio beside him. "Does that radio run on batteries too? Did you bring any?"

Ike nodded, then leaned down and turned it on.

"Still not sure of the exact time it broadcasts," he said, tuning to the station he'd memorized and sitting back against the cool cement wall. "Sometimes it's early in the morning, and sometimes it's—"

The carousel music started up.

"Here it comes!" Ike said excitedly.

"3, 9, 2, 3, 1, 4, 0, 7, 14, 38, 12 . . . EYES ONLY. S-T-A-V LAUNCH-PREP SAFETY CHECK."

Ike and Eesha both froze.

"Launch?" Ike said. "What launch?"

"What's 'S-T-A-V'?" Eesha asked.

It went on for two more minutes and then shut off. Ike took out his notebook and scribbled down the new message.

"We have to find out what it means," Eesha exclaimed.

Ike didn't know what to say.

It was quiet. Too quiet.

Eesha held up a finger. "Wait a minute," she said, a hint of anxiety in her voice. "Jack and Jill. I don't hear them."

They both rushed out of the cement mixer.

And found two strange figures standing over the twins.

Chapter Twelve

"Hey!" Eesha shouted, picking up a thick branch from the ground. "Get away from them!" She took a few steps forward. Ike followed her lead. He then remembered that he had that Swiss Army knife he'd taken from the footlocker. He pulled it from his pants pocket, but didn't unfold it.

Two people stood before them—a man and a woman. Ike studied them closely. Both wore black suits and had very pale skin. They really seemed out of place, he thought. *Who wears a black suit in the heat of summer?* He remembered his mom's warning about wearing his black T-shirt. Funny thing was, he didn't see any sign of sweat on either of them.

"Hey there, little lady," the woman started, holding up her hands. "We did not mean any harm. We were just checking on the kids. We thought they were alone."

Ike paused. There was something funny about the way

she spoke. It was kind of like the way a bad actor delivers a line in a movie. The twins looked to the strangers and then back to Eesha.

Ike saw Eesha bristle. Probably at being called "little lady."

"They're my brother and sister," she said, still holding the branch. "Back off!" Ike had no idea she could sound so threatening. "Jack. Jill. Come here."

The twins obeyed without complaint.

The man stepped forward. His bald head gleamed in the sun. Ike blinked. His skin was so white, he looked like a ghost. "What is your name, young lady? You too, son. You know this is a restricted area?"

Again, Ike's ears twitched at the stilted cadence of his voice, just like his companion's.

"Where?" Eesha challenged them. "I didn't see any signs."

But I did, Ike remembered. A rusty No Trespassing sign.

He had a decision to make. He could cooperate with these people, or they could both make a run for it. But the twins wouldn't be able to keep up. His brain was racing through different scenarios a mile a minute. "Who are you?" he finally asked.

The two strangers traded glances. "If you kids do not

want to get into trouble, I suggest you give us your names," the woman replied.

"And drop the stick," the man warned Eesha.

This was getting serious, Ike realized. His parents would ground him for weeks if they found out he was someplace he shouldn't be. He opened his mouth, and what came out of it surprised even him. "I'm . . . Zeke . . . Johnson."

He expected them to laugh and howl at the sudden declaration of a fake name, but they didn't. They only turned to Eesha and waited for her to follow "Zeke's" lead.

"I'm Jane Cabot," she put in, finally dropping the stick. The twins stood still and quiet, aware of how strange the encounter was.

"Okay," the woman said, "Miss Cabot and Mr. Johnson. You are in a restricted area. We need you to clear out."

"Immediately," the man added.

"We didn't see any signs!" Eesha challenged them.

Ike winced. He was growing more nervous by the moment. She was going to get them into trouble! "Let's go," he said nervously.

Eesha looked to him, her eyes wide. She blew out a breath and turned back to the strangers. "We told you who we are. So, who are you?"

Ike closed his eyes. His legs felt like jelly.

The two strangers looked at each other again. "You are really something, aren't you?" the woman said. "We gave you a direct order. Leave now, or we call the authorities."

Ike reached out for Eesha's arm and tugged. She shook him off and then, just like in the movies, actually spit on the ground. "C'mon," she said, reaching for Jill's hand. "We're leaving."

"That is a smart decision," the man said.

Ike cautiously walked back to the cement mixer and retrieved his backpack. It was only a few steps away, but it seemed like a mile. He stuffed the radio into it and slung it over his shoulder. The mysterious strangers eyed him as he came back out.

"C'mon," he said to Eesha.

Eesha stood a moment longer, continuing the standoff.

"Jane!" Ike shouted, relieved he had remembered her fake name.

Finally, she turned away. But not before looking back one last time and narrowing her eyes.

Chapter Thirteen

Ike's footfalls sounded as loud as dinosaur steps in his ears. Beads of sweat trembled on his brow. He waited until they were clear of the strangers before he spoke. Eesha's face was set in a hard scowl.

"We've done it now," he said.

"We didn't do anything wrong!" Eesha fumed. "Did you see any signs anywhere? I didn't. They were following us for some reason!"

Ike kept his mouth shut about the No Trespassing sign. "Good thing they didn't see the radio."

"Maybe they have a way of figuring out who's listening to that station," Eesha put in.

Ike shook his head. "Doubt it. It's low-tech, remember? How would they be able to trace it? It can't be hacked. Like you said before—no digital footprints."

Eesha nodded but didn't seem convinced. "Do you think they'll tell our parents?"

Ike scoffed. "Fake names. Remember?"

"Ah," Eesha said. "Right. That was quick thinking."

"Jane Cabot?" he ventured. "Where'd that come from?"

Eesha grinned. "She's a character in a graphic novel! Dummies didn't even know about *Amazing Jane*."

"Never heard of it," Ike confessed. "I just blurted out the first name that came into my head."

"Well, those are our secret aliases now," Eesha told him.

"The way they talked," Ike said. "It was odd. I can't put my finger on it."

"I noticed it, too. Like they were robots or something, trying to learn English."

They walked in silence for a while, the twins following behind. Ike's brain went into overdrive trying to figure out who the two suit-wearing people could be. They didn't look like military types. So, who were they?

Eesha peered around warily as she walked, as if the strangers could appear again at any moment.

"Give it back!" Jack shouted. "It's my turn now!"

"No!" Jill shot back. "I found it. It's mine!"

Ike and Eesha turned around.

"What are you talking about?" Eesha demanded. "Give what back?"

Jill looked up at her big sister. Dirt streaked her face and hands. "It's mine!" she pouted, sticking out her bottom lip. "I found it."

"Found what?" Ike asked.

Jill slowly opened her closed fist. Eesha leaned down and looked.

"What the . . . ?" Ike gasped.

Jill wiped her nose with the back of her other hand. "I didn't do nothing. I found it. It's a toy. And it's mine!"

Eesha took the object from her sister. It was round, about three inches across. A gold rim encircled it like a clock face, but instead of roman numerals or a second hand, there were strange equations. "Looks like math symbols," she said.

"They are," Eesha added. "I know them from geometry class. But what about those other little engravings?"

Ike looked closely and saw that all along the rim were several pictograms: clouds, a moon, a pyramid, a flame, wavy lines that looked like it could mean water, and many more.

A small divot was at the bottom, like your thumb was supposed to go there.

"Weird," Ike said. "Let me hold it."

Eesha handed it to him, and he held it up to the bright

sun. He squinted. A rainbow appeared in the air around it, like a prism.

"Jill, where did you find this?" Eesha asked. "Tell the truth."

Jill chewed her lip and scrunched up her face beneath the bicycle helmet. "Back there," she pointed, turning around. "Where we were playing. It was in a hole . . . in the ground."

Jack nodded along in agreement.

"This has to be something important," Eesha said. "Maybe that's why those goons said it was a restricted area."

"But what is it?" Ike demanded.

"Don't know," Eesha said, taking it back and studying it once more. "Looks like alien tech to me."

☆ ☆ ☆

Ike and Eesha couldn't agree on who should hold on to the mystery clock. In the end, Eesha won, seeing as how her sister had found it. "I'll keep it safe," she promised him. "Don't worry."

But Ike did worry.

Back home, when he opened the front door to his house, he half expected to see the two weirdos seated on the couch with his mom, patiently waiting for his arrival.

Fortunately, his parents were still at work. He went upstairs and flopped onto his bed.

There were several things they needed to figure out.

The numbers.

The mystery clock.

The disappearing footprints.

And the two black-suited strangers.

Ike sighed and stared at the ceiling. *What does it all mean?*

He drifted off to sleep and didn't wake up until his parents came home at 6 p.m.

☆ ☆ ☆

Dinner was tofu meat loaf. Ike looked at it skeptically. He picked up his fork and took a bite.

His mom studied him, waiting for his reaction. Ike was wondering if she would mention the radio again.

"Pretty good," he managed to say. It was true. It wasn't as bad as he would have thought.

"*And* it's healthy," his mom put in.

Apparently, his dad thought so too. He cleaned his plate and took another helping. "So," he said. "What'd you do today, kiddo?"

Ike swallowed another bite. He didn't want to lie, so he told a half-truth. "Just exploring with Eesha. Out in the woods looking for old arrowheads and stuff."

A smile lit up his mother's face. "Oh! I knew you two would hit it off again."

Ike just nodded. His mind was somewhere else. If those two weirdos in the woods had found out who he really was and told his parents, their reactions would have been different. He breathed a sigh of relief and finished his meat loaf.

They didn't talk much after that. Ike thought his mom seemed preoccupied, like she was nervous about something. Or was it his imagination?

That night, he had a dream that he was being chased by the mysterious duo. He was trying to run, but it was like moving through a thick river of syrup. He bolted up with his breath in his throat as they closed in on him, their faces pale and grim.

☆ ☆ ☆

Ike awoke to the sun drifting in through the window. He focused on a diagonal patch of light on the hardwood floor. Dust motes danced within it. He stared at it for a long time, trying to piece together what he and Eesha had experienced yesterday. The dream from last night still clung to his brain.

He needed to check in with Eesha to see if anything had happened with the clock thing. He picked up his phone:

> Hey

> Hey

> Anything happen with the...you know what?

> Nope. Come over though. We can try 2 figure it out.

> K

Ike sat up and leaned back against the headboard. He felt exhausted. *What am I getting myself into?*

Ten minutes later, after telling his mom he was going out exploring again, he was at Eesha's front porch. He raised his hand to knock, but the door opened to reveal her standing in front of him. "C'mon," she said, leading him inside.

"What's going on?"

Eesha didn't reply, only headed toward the basement stairs.

Ike had no idea what was happening. "Is it the clock thing?"

Eesha flipped on the light at the top of the stairs, and Ike followed. "Where are the twins?" he asked.

"Dad had a day off and took them to some water park somewhere. I told them I wasn't interested."

Ike found that strange. Whenever they had a family

outing, he *had* to go. No two ways about it.

Eesha took a seat at the table, and Ike sat next to her. "So," she started. "I think I know who they are."

"Who?"

"Those goons in the woods." She paused. "I think they were . . . Men in Black."

Ike paused. "Uh, Men in Black?"

"Yeah. I read online that they always show up around UFO and alien activity. No one really knows what they're all about. Some people think they're aliens, too. Check it out."

They spent the next twenty minutes looking at their phones. There were hundreds of memes and videos of people posing as them, even a movie from the '90s called *Men in Black*.

Ike didn't know what to think. It was definitely weird. "If those people really were Men in Black, why would they be here?"

"Don't know," Eesha said. "I read they also work with the government in some kind of psyops."

"'Psyops'?"

"Psychological operations. Like, manipulating people to believe in something. For example, working with news stations to get their point across. Take Roswell. They said it was a weather balloon when everyone knew it wasn't."

Ike paused. He knew Eesha was really into UFO stuff, but this just sounded too bizarre to believe. He searched his mind for what to say and came up blank. She was really out there with her conspiracy theories. She reached into her pocket, took out the clock, and placed it on the table.

"Has it done anything?" Ike asked.

"Nope."

They stared at the mysterious object for a moment.

"But I have been thinking about something though," Eesha finally broke the silence.

She reached into her back pocket and unfolded the piece of paper she had used to try to decipher the word search.

"These . . . letters," she started, smoothing out the paper with her hands, "are what we found when we used the radio numbers to correspond to the letters in the word-search book: T-X-L-F-N-V-L-O-Y-H-U."

"I remember," Ike said. "It doesn't make any sense."

"Right," Eesha replied. "Not . . . *yet.*"

Ike's eyebrows rose.

"What if it's double-encrypted?" she asked.

Ike stared at her blankly. He didn't know the first thing about encryption, not to mention *double* encryption.

Eesha stood up and began to pace. She walked back and forth, counting on her fingers and whispering to herself. She came to a halt and turned to him.

"What?" Ike asked, his curiosity growing by the second.

"Ike, our parents are in the military, right? Wouldn't it make sense for them to use some kind of military intelligence in sending a message?"

Ike chuckled.

"What?" Eesha said, taken aback. "What's so funny?"

"You know what my dad says?" he asked.

"Uh, no."

"He says that military intelligence is an oxymoron."

Eesha smirked. "Yeah. I've heard that one, too. What do you call an officer who goes to the bathroom a lot?"

"What?"

"A *loo*-tenant," Eesha snorted. "You know. The loo. The bathroom. That's what they called it when we were in England."

"Hilarious," Ike mocked her.

"Okay," Eesha said, standing up. "Back to it." She paused. "Did you know that one of the first encryption methods was something called the Caesar cipher, named after Julius Caesar?"

"Um, okay?"

"He used it to send commands to his generals in the field. We learned about it in Greek and Roman studies."

"I don't remember studying that," Ike admitted.

Eesha grinned. "It was an honors class."

Ike felt his face go hot. His grades weren't good enough to be in an honors class. He was a good student but didn't always push himself to study harder, as one of his teachers once said.

"So," Eesha continued, beginning to pace the room. "The Caesar cipher was simple, but if you didn't have the key, you couldn't figure it out."

"How'd it work?" Ike asked.

Eesha leaned over the table and then picked up a nearby pen. "Let's say you want to send a message to your army." She began to write on the paper and spoke the letters aloud:

"D-W-W-D-F-N."

"Now, shift each letter back," she directed him. "By . . . three."

Ike turned the paper to face him. Eesha handed him the pen. "Okay," he started. "Move each letter back by three. The first letter, D, would be an . . . A."

"Right," Eesha said.

Ike chewed his lip while he worked it out. "W would be . . ." He ran through the alphabet in his head. "T. And then T again."

"Uh-huh," Eesha encouraged him.

"D again is A," Ike continued. "F . . . is C. And N is . . . K."

"Presto," Eesha said.

Ike looked at the letters he'd just written.

A T T A C K

"Attack," he whispered. He set the pen down and leaned back in his chair. "It's so simple."

"Told you," Eesha said. She turned the paper back to face her. "These letters: T-X-L-F-N-V-L-O-Y-H-U could be in Caesar cipher. A double encryption."

"Try it!" Ike demanded. "Let's see if it works."

"Here goes," Eesha said, sitting back down opposite Ike and scribbling onto the page, every now and then counting off on her fingers.

"I'm going to move each letter back by three, just like we did before. It's the most common method for the Caesar cipher. If that doesn't work, we'll try four, then five. It might take a while."

Ike hoped it wouldn't. He watched in anticipation as Eesha continued her work, her tongue darting to the corner of her mouth in concentration. Finally, she set the pen down. She didn't move.

"Eesha?" Ike said.

Ike saw her swallow. She remained motionless.

"It's a word," she said.

Ike turned the paper around.

QUICKSILVER

"Quicksilver," he said softly.

Eesha raised her eyes from the page to meet his. "And what's another word for quicksilver?"

The answer hit Ike like a bolt of lightning. He'd learned it in science class last year. "Mercury."

Chapter Fourteen

"We were right," Eesha said. "Something's happening here, in Mercury-freakin'-Nevada!"

Ike slowly shook his head. Could it be? Did they really just prove that something top secret was going on? "INSCOM," he said quietly. "That article said they were specialists at cryptography."

"And we just cracked their freakin' code!" Eesha exclaimed.

Ike had his doubts. Was it really that simple?

"So," Eesha said, surprisingly calm. "With this discovery, the message now reads . . ." She picked up the paper. "Quicksilver eyes only . . . Report Kilo. Report Kilo."

"Kilo is a measure of weight, right?" Ike asked.

"Yeah," Eesha said. "But I don't know what that has to do with this message."

"Quicksilver eyes only," Ike said in a thoughtful tone. "Quicksilver has to be the name of the operation. No—a project. That's the word I was looking for."

Eesha nodded. "I think you're right, Ike. And eyes only means something that's intended only for certain people."

"The people on the project," Ike put in.

"Like your mom."

Ike fell silent.

"But what about the other words?" Eesha went on. "Kilo? Sierra?"

Ike rubbed his brow. "I feel like I've heard those words together before somewhere."

Eesha dug her phone out of her pocket. After a moment, she opened her mouth wide. "I don't believe it."

"What?"

"We of all people should have known, being military kids."

"*What?*" Ike persisted.

"It's ICAO code," Eesha said.

"What the heck is ICAO code?"

Eesha grinned. "You've heard it before, Ike. We've all heard it."

He let out a frustrated breath, impatient.

"Alfa," Eesha began. "Bravo. Charlie . . ."

Ike paused a moment, and then caught on. "Oh, I see. Delta. Echo. Foxtrot. Wait. I don't know what comes after that."

Eesha looked back to the computer.

"Golf," she said. "And then: Hotel. India. Juliett . . ." She hesitated, as if for dramatic effect. *"Kilo."*

Ike was dumbstruck.

"It's ICAO code," Eesha repeated. "It stands for International Civil Aviation Organization!"

Ike had a memory of being a kid, playing army with his friends. They used to run around shouting these words because they'd heard them in action movies and TV shows.

A flash at the corner of his vision drew his eyes away from Eesha.

A red glow encircled the rim of the clockface.

"Oh my god," Eesha whispered.

"Shh," Ike exclaimed, leaning in to get a closer look.

"It's . . . it's changing colors!" Eesha cried out.

The clockface rim went from red to green to a ghostly blue.

"What do we do?" Ike said, his voice trembling a little. He watched in fascination as it faded to a deep purple. It reminded him of a lava lamp. His parents had one, and he liked how the colors swirled around in it. "Do you think it's dangerous? It could be radioactive or something."

Eesha reached out her hand.

"Don't!" he warned her.

But she did.

Ike held his breath.

"Feels . . . normal," she said. "Here."

She handed it to him. He tentatively took it and weighed it in his palm. It was cool to the touch, slowly pulsing purple. He set it back down on the table between them, and they continued to gaze at it.

"We have to go back," Eesha said absently, as if entranced.

"Where?" Ike asked.

"To where the twins found it."

Ike stood up. "The cement mixer? You're nuts! What if we see those freaks in black again? What then?"

"There has to be another clue," Eesha persisted, chewing a fingernail. "I mean, why was it there? They said it was a restricted area. Why? *Why* is it restricted? Maybe they were looking for this . . . whatever it is."

Ike sat back down and put his head in his hands. Eesha's questions were the same as his. This was getting serious. But she had a point, no matter how dangerous it sounded. They were finally onto something. He couldn't back down now. *That's what . . . friends do*, he thought. *Stick together through thick and thin.*

"Okay," he said. "We'll go. But if we hear or see anyone, we gotta hightail it out of there."

Eesha swiped the clock from the table and put it in her pocket.

☆ ☆ ☆

Eesha walked quickly, with long, determined strides. Ike had to move twice as fast to keep up with her. It was still early, and songbirds chirped in the trees. Sprinklers ticked on, beginning their morning rotations. The sun was not yet at its high point, and they took a little relief in that.

Ike wondered if they were doing the right thing. If they got caught, he couldn't even imagine what his parents would do. Could a kid be grounded for eternity?

Quicksilver, he thought. *Mercury*.

And that's when it hit him.

He came to a halt.

"Eesha," he called. She was still a few steps ahead of him.

She turned around. "Yeah?"

Ike searched for the right words. "I . . . I just realized it. I was so excited back there, it didn't really hit me until now. *Quicksilver*. That message was from my mom's word-search book. Those numbers from the radio station were meant for her! It's a . . . she's a . . . spy or something!"

Eesha moved closer and placed a hand on his shoulder. Ike adjusted his glasses.

"I know it's a shock," she consoled him. "But we were right, Ike. Something's happening. Something . . . secret. There's no going back now." She paused, her face stoic.

"You're going to have to act normal around her from here on out."

Ike knew it was true. He had to be even more of a sneak. He felt awful. How was his mom involved in all of this? Now he knew why she was always scribbling in her word-search books. She was receiving secret messages! And how was she getting them? Did she have another radio hidden away somewhere? The reality of it was overwhelming. Ike tried to control his thoughts, but his mind had other plans—and the questions kept coming.

What would he do when they finally found the answer? *Depends on what those answers are*, he thought to himself.

As they continued to walk, he spied the main gate to the base in the distance. He half expected an alarm to sound, followed by a convoy of military police trucks encircling them, sirens blaring and lights flashing. He could even imagine what it sounded like. *Freeze! Hands on your heads!*

But no such thing happened. There was only a barking dog and the sound of two kids shouting and playing catch on their front lawn. Eesha seemed caught up in her own thoughts, and he didn't ask her any more questions. She was probably just as freaked out as he was. He had a sudden thought. And it had to be said.

"Eesha?"

"Yeah?"

"Do you . . . do you think we should tell our parents what we found?"

She immediately came to a stop and turned to face him on the sidewalk. She cocked her head. "Why would we do that?"

Ike stared at his sneakers and then raised his head again. "I'm just trying to be honest. Lay out the options. What if the clock is some kind of military device? We could get into a lot of trouble if we're caught with it, especially after those . . . Men in Black told us to clear out."

Eesha slowly shook her head, a slight smile on her face. "Ike, you're what my parents would call a 'good kid,' and you want to do the right thing, whatever that is. But we're *onto* something. Something *big*. If we get in trouble, well, that's just the price we'll have to pay." She drew a little closer to him and lowered her voice. "Don't you want to find out what this is all about? The clock and the base opening back up? The numbers? It's all connected. I don't care if I *do* get in trouble. It'll be worth it if we find out what's really going on."

Ike bit his lip. She was right. He'd always done the right thing in his life. Followed the rules. Obeyed his parents. But something inside of him was urging him on. He had to take a chance. *I have to know the truth*, he thought. *Once and for all.*

"Okay," he said, releasing a heavy breath. "I'm in. But we have to stick together if we're caught, right?"

Eesha grinned. "One hundred percent."

The cement mixer wasn't far, but the walk seemed like a thousand miles to Ike. It was on the base, of course, but in the woods, in an area far from military housing. He felt like he was sleepwalking, his legs as heavy as if he were wearing lead boots. *My mom's a spy. A spy! Whose side is she on?*

The voice in his head was loud and persistent. This wasn't a fantasy story or conspiracy theory. It was real.

Finally, the edge of the woods appeared, and they made their way into the forest. Ike stared into the dense thicket of trees. He swallowed. "Here we go."

Chapter Fifteen

Ike and Eesha walked warily. The sun was brighter now, but the dense canopy of leaves and the snarl of tree branches overhead blocked the hot rays. Ike saw the cement mixer ahead of them and, for a quick moment, expected to see the two strangers come rushing out.

"Where did the twins find it?" Ike asked, as they drew closer to it, stepping carefully, trying to avoid snapping branches and crunching leaves.

"They were over here," Eesha said. "This is where those Men in Black were talking to them."

Men in Black, Ike thought, even though one of them was a woman. *Women in Black?* His world had been turned upside down.

Eesha knelt down and dug her fingers around in the soil. Ike did the same, only to get dirt under his fingernails.

"Uh-oh," Eesha said.

Ike froze.

Eesha was staring at the ground. "Look," she said, pointing.

Ike slowly walked the few steps to where she stood and looked down.

Tracks. Footprints. Just like the ones he'd seen before.

"So strange," Eesha said. She knelt down and put her fingers in the impression. "Ouch!" she suddenly cried out, darting back up.

"What?" Ike said, alarmed.

Eesha danced on her toes while digging into her pocket.

"What are you doing?"

She quickly withdrew the clockface and dropped it to the ground, then raised her hand to her mouth to suck her fingers.

"It burned!" she cried. "It was getting hot! I could feel it through my shorts!"

Ike and Eesha stared at the clock. The rim around it glowed a fiery red.

"Why?" Ike asked. "Why would it do that?"

"No idea," Eesha said, rubbing her fingers.

"We can't leave it here," Ike put in.

"I know. Maybe it'll cool down in a second."

They both continued to observe the clock. Ike wanted to poke it with a stick but hesitated. He was wondering if it would catch fire or something. He jumped as a flash appeared several feet in front of him.

He threw himself to the ground. "Get down!"

"What?" Eesha said at full volume, whipping her head left and then right.

Ike reached up and grasped her hand, pulling her to the forest floor.

"What are you—?" she protested, spitting a leaf from her mouth.

"Shh," Ike cut her off. "I saw something. Over there." He pointed ahead.

They both stared into the woods.

The sound of breaking branches cracked as loud as thunder. Ike shuddered. *I knew we shouldn't have come back. Darn it! The Men in Black are going to find us!*

"It's coming this way!" Eesha whisper-shouted. She bolted to her feet, pulling Ike up at the same time. "Run!"

Ike didn't have time to think. The Men in Black were after them, and he and Eesha were going to be arrested. Or worse.

They took off, crashing through the trees, trying to find the path. Ike's heart raced in his chest, hammering his insides. Branches scratched his face, but he kept moving. *Mom's going to kill me. I'll be grounded forever. Or even go to jail! What if she's working with the Russians or something? I'll be shipped off to one of those . . . Russian gulag prisons I read about in school!*

"Wait!" a voice shouted.

A *kid's* voice.

Eesha skidded to a stop, breathing hard. Ike did the same, almost falling over a rotting log.

They both turned around.

A girl stood in front of them. She wore a purple jumpsuit and looked to be around the same age as them.

"Hi," she said. "I'm Mixie."

Ike and Eesha stood frozen.

The girl, Mixie, was as tall as Eesha, with bright green eyes and a pleasant face framed by pink, pixie-cut hair. It almost looked like a wig. It had a plastic sheen to it, and one curl stuck to her forehead as if it had been glued there. Her jumpsuit seemed to be reflective and dazzled in the bright sunlight.

Mixie sniffed the air, her small nostrils flaring. "I can sense my theorem equalizer. Do you have it? I seem to have lost it."

Ike and Eesha continued to stare at her, both of them breathing hard.

"Where . . ." Ike started. "What is a . . . Where did you come from?"

Mixie laughed, a light tinkling sound. She turned

around and pointed into the trees. "Through there."

"The woods?" Eesha asked.

In answer, Mixie cocked her head, a small finger pointing into the air. "Wait . . . what year is it?"

"What *year*?" Eesha asked.

When Ike told Mixie, she laughed and shook her head. "I had no idea I could go back that far," she said, as if in awe.

"What do you mean?" Ike asked.

"Don't you see?" Mixie said excitedly. "I traveled into the past. I'm from the year 3000!"

Chapter Sixteen

It took a moment for Ike and Eesha to process what Mixie had just said. They both stared at her, mouths agape.

"The year . . . *3000*?" Ike finally uttered.

"Yes," Mixie replied, continuing to peer around the forest. "I'm from your future. We read about your history in school!"

Eesha opened her mouth, but no words came out. A squirrel skittered down a tree, nails scrabbling on the trunk. Mixie turned at the sound and watched it run along the forest floor. "Genus *Sciurus*," she whispered. "They're extinct in my time."

She crept a little closer, studying it. "To see it in its own natural habitat is—"

"Get down!" Eesha whispered.

"What?" Ike said. "What is it?"

"They're back!" Eesha warned him. "I saw movement in the trees!"

Mixie turned away from the squirrel. "Who?" she asked.

"Bad people," Eesha said in a low voice. "Men in Black. We have to hide! Get down!"

Mixie looked around as if she hadn't a care in the world. "Do you have my theorem equalizer?" she asked again.

Eesha blew out a frustrated breath. "What is a— I don't know what you're talking about!"

"It looks like what you would call a . . . clock?" Mixie explained. "It should be hot by now. The closer I get, the warmer it becomes."

A murmur of voices floated through the trees. Eesha's eyes went wide.

"Give it to her!" Ike said, a little too loudly.

"*You* give it to her! I'm not touching that thing again!"

Ike huffed and scrambled over on his hands and knees to where Eesha had dropped it. "It's right here," he called. "Hurry!"

Mixie ambled over—seemingly in no hurry—picked it up and closed her hands around it. Slivers of red light began to glow between her fingers. She held her closed hands up to her mouth and whispered.

And then, something remarkable happened.

They were surrounded by a pulsating red glow, as if

they had just stepped into a giant bubble. "There," Mixie said. "That should do it."

"Do what?" Eesha asked. "We have to get out of here!"

"They won't be able to see or hear us now," Mixie explained. "It's a cloaking device. And a lot of other things, too. Go ahead. Stand up. I promise they won't see you."

Eesha pushed herself up from the ground. Ike stared in disbelief as the mysterious duo stepped out of the woods and walked toward them. He closed his eyes in fear, but what he heard them say was beyond belief.

"Where did they go?" the woman asked, dumbfounded.

"I thought I heard voices," the man replied in a monotone voice.

They continued their search, studying the ground for footprints, Ike assumed. He tried to form words but was having a hard time. "This is . . . What is . . . happ . . ."

Eesha crouched, pressed her palms up against the bubble, and stared. "Remarkable. Impossible. They really can't see or hear us!"

"Wait until I tell Flax and Silver," Mixie said. "They won't believe this!"

Ike stared at the girl called Mixie. *Weird name*, he thought. Weirder still, she said she was from the future.

How was it possible?

Finally, after what seemed an eternity, the intruders

turned to one another, said something Ike couldn't hear, and went back in the direction they came, walking in a strangely clumsy fashion.

The shock of what Ike and Eesha had just experienced left them silent. "Okay . . . Mixie," Ike finally said. "Can you get us out of here?"

"Sure."

She raised her hand and . . . poked a finger into the protective red bubble.

Ike felt a *pop* in his ears, like when you're flying and reach a high altitude. The bubble vanished. "Maximum, isn't it?"

Ike and Eesha shared a confused glance.

"*Maximum?*" Eesha repeated.

Mixie cocked her head. "Maximum. It means . . . how would you say it? Cool?"

"Ah," Ike said. "Yeah. Cool."

Mixie smiled. "We studied a lot of old Earth slang in school."

Ike felt as if he were in a dream. He had just met a girl from the future who had a magic clock.

"We've got questions," Eesha said, pulling a twig from her hair. "So many questions."

Chapter Seventeen

"We better get outta here," Eesha said, still alarmed. "They might be back."

"Where to?" Ike put in. "And what about—?" He cocked his head in the general direction of Mixie.

Eesha released a heavy breath. "No one'll be home at my place for a while. Let's go there and try to figure it out."

Ike thought it was as good a plan as any.

Mixie followed them out of the woods, staring at every tree, rock, and flower as if studying them for future recall.

Ike and Eesha walked in a daze until Ike finally spoke up. "So," he started. "You said you traveled into our past. How did you . . . how did you get here? Time machine?"

"Ah," Mixie said. "It's a bit more complicated than that."

And then she began to talk.

And talk.

And talk.

Ike didn't understand all of it. She told them about the second law of thermodynamics, Einstein's general theory of relativity, time dilation, and wormholes—which she called an Einstein-Rosen bridge.

"So," she said. "It really does work, but we're not supposed to use it. Our elders say we could mess things up in your time if we did."

"Then why did you come?" Eesha asked. "And why here?"

Mixie paused, her face as guilty as the cat who ate all the cream. "I was just . . . fooling around. I wanted to see if I could really do it." She paused. "In our time, we learned there are certain . . . frequencies—portals, we call them— that can bridge the distances between time."

Ike halted in his tracks, which led Mixie and Eesha to do the same.

"Portals?" Ike questioned her.

"I don't know what else to call them," Mixie replied.

"So, there's a portal here?" Eesha asked. "In Mercury? That's how you came through?"

"Yes," Mixie said. "Back there in the forest. I slipped through a few days ago, but I didn't explore. I was a little afraid. That's when I lost my theorem equalizer. So, I had to come back for it, and that's when I saw you two!"

Ike and Eesha stared at each other. Something beyond their imagination was happening. *Portals*, Ike thought. *Unbelievable.*

They continued to walk, leaving the woods behind and arriving back at base housing. Mixie continued to stare at everything. "So," she said. "Are you in school? What do you study? How old are you?"

Ike and Eesha answered her simple questions with patience. It felt so strange. She was from the future! Ike still couldn't wrap his head around it, and her brainiac explanation about time travel didn't help, either.

A question suddenly formed in his head. He was surprised neither he nor Eesha had asked yet.

"So, you said you were from our future. What . . . what happens to us? The people of Earth? In our time?"

Mixie's pleasant demeanor suddenly shifted. "Oh," she started, as if surprised by the question. "I'm not sure I'm supposed to say. Remember when I said that time travel could have an impact on things?"

Eesha nodded. "But Earth is still here, right? We didn't blow ourselves up or anything?"

Ike felt a sudden pang of anxiety. "Or destroyed the planet with global warming?"

Mixie's eyes swept the ground. It was the first time Ike

had seen her look uncomfortable. "I . . . I really shouldn't say."

A cloak of sadness seemed to settle on Ike's shoulders. Eesha's face was grim as well.

"I *can* say, however," Mixie continued, bringing Ike back to the moment, "that the future lies in the stars." She pointed a finger into the air.

"So, we become a spacefaring species?" Ike asked breathlessly.

Mixie didn't answer, only smiled in the affirmative.

They didn't speak again until they were standing in front of Eesha's door.

☆ ☆ ☆

"Hello?" Eesha called, stepping into her living room. Ike and Mixie followed her. "Dad? Nerd-bots?"

No answer.

"Must still be at the water park," she said.

Mixie glanced around the room. "Ah, you have a television! I saw one of these in a museum! Can you turn it on?"

Eesha glanced at Ike. They were both flabbergasted. She picked up the remote and turned the power on. The screen lit up and revealed a cartoon.

Mixie walked over and put her face only inches away. "Old-school," she said. "That's another one of my favorite slang phrases from your time."

"What do you have?" Ike asked. "In the future? To watch stuff on?"

"Oh, we have holograms," Mixie replied. "It's called Virtual Sky. It's like being in the same environment with the actors or musicians. It's really maximum."

"Cool," Ike whispered. "Like virtual reality or something. There's a lot of stuff in our world getting close to that tech."

"Follow me," Eesha said quickly, leading them down to the basement.

They all took seats, Eesha on the couch and Ike in one of the chairs. Mixie planted herself in the beanbag. She bounced up and down like a child.

"So," Eesha started. "Do you mind if we ask you some more questions?"

"Sure," Mixie said. "Fire away."

Eesha glanced to Ike before she spoke. "You said you came here through a portal. What is that, exactly?"

Mixie's happy expression suddenly turned to one of guilt. "We're not supposed to go near the portals if we find one. They're dangerous. I was being . . . mischievous, my parents would say. Especially my dad. He's a bit . . . excitable. But I just had to explore. I love exploring!"

Ike smiled. He knew where she was coming from.

"So, you're not supposed to use portals?" Eesha asked.

Mixie sighed. "No. We're not. Where I come from, every kid is told the story of Poor Nico."

"Nico?" Ike repeated.

"Yes. Poor Nico. It's like, what would you call it? A fable? A parable?"

"What happened to him?" Eesha asked.

"He was out walking once and found a glowing opening between two trees. He knew he wasn't supposed to go any farther. He should have turned around and told his parents, but he didn't. Instead, he walked into it and never came out again. And that's the story of Poor Nico."

Ike nodded, a little disturbed.

"Portals are easy to spot if you have the right tools," Mixie explained. "Do you want to see?"

Ike and Eesha didn't even have to reply.

Mixie reached into a fold in her jumpsuit and took out the theorem equalizer.

"Now," she began, "I need element thirteen. Do you have any?"

"What . . . is element thirteen?" Eesha asked.

But Ike already knew the answer. "That's aluminum, right?"

"Yes!" Mixie said gleefully.

"I don't think we have any of that around here," Eesha said.

"Yes, you do," countered Ike. "Foil. Aluminum foil. It's a conductor of electricity!"

Mixie looked perplexed. "What is foil?"

Ike slapped his hand over his mouth before he could laugh.

"Be right back," Eesha announced, and then dashed upstairs.

Ike felt a little weird sitting alone with Mixie. She was a future human. *Imagine the stuff she knows*, he thought. What was her world—our world—like?

"So," Mixie said, breaking the silence. "You and Eesha. You are best friends?"

Ike adjusted his glasses. "Well, um. Yeah, we're friends."

Ike couldn't exactly put into words how he felt about Eesha. They did do everything best friends would do, after all. Come to think of it, he realized, they were. "Yeah," he said again. "I guess you could say that."

Mixie smiled, showing perfect rows of white teeth. "Silver and Flax are my best friends, back home. I can't wait to tell them about my adventure!"

Odd names, Ike thought. *Flax. Silver. Mixie.* He wanted to know more about her world, but couldn't think of the right questions just yet.

The sound of Eesha bounding back down the stairs drew their attention. She was carrying a roll of aluminum foil. Mixie stared at it as if she were looking at an artifact in a museum. Eesha unrolled it and tore off a sheet along the sharp little teeth.

"Fascinating," Mixie said, her fingers lightly touching the foil, an air of wonder in her voice.

She took the sheet, laid it on the table, then set the theorem equalizer on top of the foil. Sparks immediately ignited around it. Ike and Eesha stepped back, wary. They'd seen what the theorem equalizer did earlier. Who knew what else it could do?

"Ah, there we go," Mixie said. "This . . . *foil* is really ingenious!"

"Yeah," Eesha said, hiding a chuckle. "It is."

"Now it's charged," Mixie said. "So. What do you call this place? Where we are?"

"America?" Ike suggested.

"More specific," Mixie demanded.

"Nevada," Eesha put in. "Mercury, Nevada."

Mixie nodded. "Show me satellite images. Mercury, Nevada."

Ike and Eesha watched in fascination as the round clocklike theorem equalizer suddenly expanded and formed a square, like a computer screen, and then went dark. Tiny nodules of lights, like fireflies, blinking on and off, appeared within the screen.

"Cool," Eesha whispered. "Kind of like our Google Maps."

But what happened next really surprised them.

A 3D hologram of the United States rose from the table and spun around, letting the viewer see it from all sides. Ike saw the topography in clear detail: towering mountain ranges, the vast expanse of oceans. "This is . . ."

"Maximum?" Eesha suggested.

"Yeah," Ike whispered. "Totally maximum."

Mixie swiped the screen like one would do on a tablet, and the images became more focused. There was the military base, the forest, their neighborhood.

"This should show us the portal I came through," Mixie explained. "Show me cosmic strings, gateways. Anything emitting time dilation."

Ike shook his head in amazement at Mixie's scientific jargon.

The images grew even more magnified until it closed in on an area highlighted with a blinking red light.

"Oh," Mixie said. "There's the one I came through." She paused. "Hmm. Looks like there's another one."

Ike and Eesha leaned in toward the 3D image.

Mixie was right.

There was another blinking red light.

And it was on the army base.

Chapter Eighteen

"It's on the army base," Ike whispered.

"Yes," Mixie said. "Fascinating. Two portals so close to each other means they lead to the same space-time continuum. Our scientists discovered that decades ago."

Ike felt as if his head had exploded. He was sure Eesha felt the same.

Silence filled the room.

Mixie's tablet screen winked out.

"We have to show you something," Eesha blurted out. She turned to Ike, sitting next to her. "Show her the numbers. The ones in your book."

"Ah," Ike said, picking his backpack up from the floor. He rooted around in it and pulled out his notebook. Mixie leaned in as he turned the pages. "We got this message from an old radio. It was a bunch of numbers that we figured out. '3, 9, 2, 3, 1, 4, 0, 7, 14, 38, 12 . . . EYES ONLY. S-T-A-V. LAUNCH-PREP SAFETY CHECK.' Do you know what any of this means?"

Mixie chewed her lip for a moment, thinking. "Hmm," she murmured. "Well, the numbers spell out 'Quicksilver' in simple Caesar cipher."

Ike looked at Eesha as if to say, *Where was she when we needed her?*

"And the other part?" Ike asked. "The letters 'S-T-A-V'?"

Mixie shook her head. "I'm sorry, Ike. I don't know what that could mean. But 'launch-prep safety check' sounds exactly like what it says."

"A launch of some kind," Ike said.

"That's my guess," Mixie put in.

"*And* there's a portal on the base," Eesha said. She paused and turned to Ike.

"Sounds like someone is preparing to go through," Mixie said. "But who?"

Ike gulped.

"My mom," he said, his voice trembling. "My mom's gonna go through one of those portals. I just know it!" *Poor Nico*, he thought with dread.

"We don't know that for sure yet," Eesha tried to reassure him.

Ike swallowed a lump in his throat. "What if it's not safe. She might—"

Eesha laid a hand on Ike's shoulder. He was taken

aback for a moment, but turned and looked at her. "Whatever they're doing, I'm sure she's going to be safe, Ike."

But Ike didn't buy it.

"If it was safe, she would've told us about it by now. Me and Dad. It's a top secret mission because it's dangerous!"

Mixie watched the whole exchange with compassionate eyes. "Your mother, she is a flier?"

"Flier?" Ike ventured. "What do you mean?"

"A flier," Mixie repeated. "That's what we call them in my time. People and ships who go through portals to study other time periods."

Eesha shook her head in bewilderment. "You mean you have ships that go through these portals? Like UFOs?"

"What's a UFO?" Mixie asked.

"Unidentified flying object," Ike told her.

"But now they call them UAPs," Eesha clarified. "Unidentified aerial phenomena."

"We just call them crafts or long- or short-distance aerials," Mixie replied.

Ike couldn't believe what he was hearing. "I thought you said that your people couldn't interfere with the past?"

"They don't," Mixie said. "They only study and observe. We've been coming here for years, all the way back from, let's see"—she counted on her fingers—"since your 1950s."

"Wait a minute," Eesha started. "That means that all

the UFOs that people have been seeing for years aren't from other planets?"

"They're us," Ike said. "From our own future."

"That's one way of saying it," Mixie said.

Ike thought of all the research he had done on UFOs, Roswell, and other events. Could it have all been future humans?

A door slammed upstairs, and the sound reverberated through his body.

Eesha gasped. "My dad. And the twins!"

"What do we do?" Ike burst out.

"Eesha," Mr. Webb's voice boomed. "We're back."

Chapter Nineteen

Ike heard the clomping of small feet on the stairs, and the twins rushed down, both of them stuffing their faces with swirls of cotton candy. They stared intently at Ike and Mixie.

"You have funny hair," Jill said, her mouth full.

"It's pink!" Jack added. "Like cotton candy!"

Mixie studied the twins as if they were some form of extinct hominid. "Well, hello!" she exclaimed. "And who are you two?"

"Uh, they're going back upstairs," Eesha cut her off, corralling them with her arms as if she were herding sheep. "We'll be up in a minute," she told them. "Now, run along, okay?"

Ike was shocked at Eesha's calmness. Maybe it was because Mixie was here, and she didn't want to look mean in front of her. Usually, she would have called them "little nerd-bots" and told them to get lost.

The twins obeyed, turning back once to stare at Mixie, who winked.

Eesha let out an exasperated sigh after the door closed behind them. "Right," she started. "I'm going to tell my dad you're a friend from the neighborhood. Okay, Mixie?"

"Do you think that'll work?" Ike asked doubtfully.

"Has to," Eesha replied.

Mixie smiled. "Okay."

They cautiously walked up the steps and into the kitchen. Eesha's dad pulled his head from the refrigerator and rose back up, an orange in his hand.

Mixie's eyes went wide. But she wasn't looking at Eesha's dad.

"Is that . . . is that an orange?" she asked, her voice full of wonder.

Mr. Webb gave Mixie a curious look. "Sure is. A *Valencia* orange, to be precise. I like to keep them cold." He looked to Eesha and then back to Mixie, who was still laser-focused on the fruit. "And who might you be?"

"I'm Mixie."

"Mixie? Well, that's certainly an unusual name. Where was your family stationed before?"

"She's new here, Dad," Eesha interrupted. "Actually, she's late for, um, her . . . French class."

"Summer school?" Mr. Webb exclaimed. "Ouch. Mon Dieu! Better take this to get your blood sugar up."

He tossed the orange, and Mixie caught it deftly. She cradled it in both hands as if it were as precious as gold, then raised it to her nose and sniffed.

"Thank you!" she said in awe. "I can't wait to try it!"

Mr. Webb looked to Eesha as if to say, *Who is this person and what is wrong with her?*

"We gotta go," Eesha blurted out.

Mixie opened her mouth to speak but was quickly dragged away by Eesha, with Ike close behind.

"Bye, Ike!" Mr. Webb shouted to their retreating backs. "À bientôt, Mixie!"

The door banged shut. They stood on the front porch in silence.

"All right," Eesha finally said, looking at Ike and Mixie. "What now?"

Mixie began to peel the orange, as carefully as if she were unwrapping a present and trying to save the paper.

"Don't you have oranges in the future?" Ike asked, offering his hand for Mixie's orange peel.

"Thank you," Mixie said, breaking off a section and handing him the peel. "Well, kind of. They're grown and harvested under artificial conditions. I've never had a real one."

Ike found that sad. He shook his head.

Mixie popped the wedge of orange into her mouth. She closed her eyes and slowly chewed.

"Mmm," she murmured. "So sweet!"

"Maximum," Eesha said.

"Okay," Ike said. "What's next?"

Mixie opened her eyes. "I must get back. My parents will worry. I have to get to the portal."

Ike's eyes went wide. "In the woods?"

"It's not safe," Eesha warned her. "Those . . . Men in Black might be there."

Mixie only shrugged. "I can use my theorem equalizer for stealth mode."

"Will we see you again?" Eesha asked.

"Sure," Mixie said. "That's easy." She popped the remainder of the orange into her mouth and then reached into one of the many hidden folds of her jumpsuit. She pulled out an object about the size of a playing card. It was deep black with a lustrous, glossy sheen. She handed it to Eesha. "If you want to reach me, tap the screen twice. It'll tell you what to do from there."

"What is it?" Eesha asked, turning the strange card in her hand.

"We call them galactic passports. Easy way to communicate across galaxies and time periods."

Sure, Ike thought. *Why not? Just another wonder from the future.*

Mixie took out the theorem equalizer and pressed her thumb into the divot. "Navigation history," she said.

"Gathering data," a pleasant voice chimed.

"Okay," Mixie said. "I should be on my way. Nice to meet you both. Thanks for showing me around!"

And then she turned and headed down the sidewalk, as carefree as if she were going to the corner store.

Ike and Eesha watched her walk away in silence.

"This is . . ." Ike started.

"Don't even try to put it into words," Eesha said.

Chapter Twenty

Ike and Eesha had so much to talk about they didn't know where to start: the arrival of Mixie and her theorem equalizer, the footprints, narrowly escaping the two mysterious strangers, being wrapped in a protective red bubble, all the information about time travel and portals. And, most worrying of all, Ike's theory that his mom might be preparing to go through one. *But why?* he wondered.

They were both too exhausted to sort it all out now. They stood on Eesha's porch in the sweltering heat. Ike wiped his forehead.

"Remember," Eesha told him before he headed home. "You have to be careful around your mom. Don't let her get more suspicious. We'll meet up tomorrow and figure out next steps."

Ike heard his friend, but her voice was muffled. She may as well have been speaking underwater. He couldn't focus, so he nodded along as if he understood and then turned to leave. But not before handing her Mixie's orange peels.

☆ ☆ ☆

Ike's head was spinning. There was just too much going on for him to comprehend. They'd met a future human! There were two portals!

He continued to walk, one step at a time, his thoughts racing. He passed the base swimming pool and heard the shouts of children and the splashing of water. The smell of chlorine rose in his nostrils.

What would he say to his mom when he saw her? He had to play it cool. He thought back to when he first saw Eesha at the state park. *I'm going to find out if UFOs and aliens are real*, she'd said.

"They are real," Ike whispered. "And they're us."

He opened the front door and stepped inside. The house was quiet. It was late afternoon, and his parents had yet to arrive home from work. Ike was relieved. He wasn't ready to deal with his mom yet. She'd probably see in his face that something was troubling him. Parents were like that. It was like a superpower or something.

He filled a glass with cold water and drank it all in one big gulp, then put the glass in the sink.

Upstairs, he sat at his desk. He didn't know what to do. *Shadow Goons* wasn't calling him to play.

He searched for "future human" on his phone, which came back as a rock band. "Portals" led to a million results and articles, most of them having nothing to do with time travel, except for in sci-fi books.

He put his earbuds in and scrolled through his playlists. He'd recently discovered a composer called Erik Satie who he really liked. The pieces were all solo piano. They were kind of quiet and melancholy, but there was something about them that he found uplifting, too. He flopped onto his bed and leaned his head back against the headboard. The music seemed to let him drift away. He imagined he was on a small white boat in a calm ocean, the water lapping at the sides, gently rocking . . .

Ike woke with a start. An hour had passed. He took out his earbuds and rubbed his eyes. He gathered his thoughts, clearing the cobwebs from his mind. In the midst of everything that had just happened, he thought about the radio and the numbers station. The radio was under his bed, so he got down on his knees and pulled it out. He carried it to his desk and turned it on. Static crackled and continued for several minutes, giving him time to ponder more questions.

Did his dad know about what his mom was doing? He had to. Ike imagined they shared everything. More questions wormed their way into his brain:

Why was his mom going?

What was the mission?

Was she going alone?

And where, exactly, *was* she going? To Mixie's time period? She'd said that two portals close to each other led to the same place.

But he also realized that he could be wrong about all of this. His mom was doing something secret, that was certain. Those letters that spelled out Quicksilver had come out of her word-search book. That had to mean something. But did it mean she was about to go through some strange portal on the base?

The carousel music started up on the radio, bringing Ike back to the moment. He felt a quick pang of anxiety. It wasn't just weird music anymore. It was a message meant for his mom.

"3, 9, 2, 3, 1, 4, 0, 7, 14, 38, 12 . . . EYES ONLY. Report Sierra."

Ike chewed his lip. The numbers were the same as before—he had them memorized by this point—but he still didn't know what Kilo and Sierra meant. He had to find out. He needed to act! If his mom was going on a secret mission, he had to make sure she was safe.

Oh man, he thought. *This is really happening!*

Chapter Twenty-One

There was no way for Ike to avoid dinner with his parents. He really just wanted to stay in his room and not have to talk to them. But that was impossible. He had to face his mom, sooner or later.

Downstairs, he found an unexpected treat. Dad had brought home pizza. His mom must have run out of health food.

"Hey, sleepyhead," she greeted him as he walked into the kitchen. "I peeked into your room and saw you sleeping so I left you alone."

His dad picked up a slice of pepperoni. "Napping during the day? How old are you, Ike, fifty?"

Ike reached for a slice with mushrooms. "Just tired," he said. "Been doing a lot of exploring lately."

"Exploring again?" Ike's mom said in astonishment. "You really are quite the adventurer, Ike."

Yeah, he thought wryly. *If you only knew the half of it.*

163

They ate their pizza while Ike's dad told a story about how a man at his office was convinced some sports team was going to win the Super Bowl, or World Series, or whatever. His voice floated in the air around him like nonsense words.

Just as Ike got up to get some crushed red pepper from the cabinet, a sound cut through his dad's voice.

It was the carousel music.

Ike froze, rooted to the spot.

He'd left the radio on in his room!

He'd always made sure he turned it off after each use and stowed it under his bed.

His mom's eyes went wide for a moment.

His dad stopped mid-chew.

Ike's mother got up and walked calmly to the couch. She picked up her purse. Ike watched closely, all the while trying to appear disinterested. But inside, his heart was racing.

He watched as his mother reached inside the purse. The music switched off. She turned around. "Work," she explained, coming back to sit down. Her face seemed to have gone pale. "They're making us all use the same ringtone now. Military regulations." She rolled her eyes and tried to make a joke out of it, but Ike didn't buy it.

Mr. Pressure relaxed his shoulders. "Ha!" he said, with a forced laugh. "That's the military for you!"

He knows, too, Ike realized. *They both know and never told me anything!*

"Ike?" his mom said. "Are you okay? You look like you've seen a ghost."

No, Ike wanted to say. *I haven't seen a ghost. I've seen a future human and a portal on the army base and a device called a theorem equalizer that can do magic.*

He swallowed the bite of mushroom pizza that seemed to be stuck in his throat, and then reached for his glass of water. He took a long swallow. "I'm okay," he said. "Just still tired."

His mom reached across the small table and placed her hand on his forehead. "You do feel a little warm."

"Hope you're not getting one of those summer colds," his dad added.

"Can I be excused?" Ike asked. "Gonna go lay down again."

"Sure, honey," his mom said in a sympathetic tone.

Ike pushed back his chair and stood up.

He could have sworn that he felt both of his parents' eyes on his back as he walked up the stairs.

Now Ike knew how his mom was getting the messages. She had some kind of secret phone for it. She probably slipped up and had forgotten it was in her purse. Maybe she was nervous and agitated about the upcoming launch.

Ike drifted in and out of dreams that night. In one, he was with Mixie, looking up at a deep purple sky filled with glowing stars. It reminded him of the pictures he'd seen of the northern lights, ghostly ribbons of color streaking the heavens. There seemed to be too many stars. Too many clusters. "Does it always look like this?" he'd asked Mixie. But he didn't get an answer, only woke up covered in sweat.

Downstairs in the morning, his mom and dad went about their tasks as if everything was normal. But Ike knew it wasn't. His mom was going on a dangerous mission, leaving him and his dad behind.

He battled with himself over whether to say something. *I could just come out and tell her I found out. Then she'd have to tell me all about it. But then I'd be in big trouble. BIG trouble. I'd have to spill the beans about Mixie and portals and Men in Black.*

No, he finally realized. Best to stay quiet. For now. He stared into his bowl of cold cereal.

His mom ambled about the kitchen. She watered the

hanging plant above the sink and hummed to herself. *Was she nervous?* Ike wondered.

"Busy day today," she said, turning from the window. "Gotta run." She set down the watering can and gave him a quick peck on the cheek. The next thing he knew, she was headed out the door with his dad.

Ike sat in silence for a moment. He took out his phone to text Eesha. They couldn't go to the cement mixer. It was compromised. Instead, Ike suggested they meet behind the school. He had to tell her how to get there. Being part of a new family on the base, and it being summer vacation, she hadn't even seen it yet. Ike had discovered it on one of his earlier expeditions.

The school wasn't too far from Ike's house, so he walked. He saw the same familiar sights, but today it was like looking at them through a smoky fog. All around him, people went about their routines, not knowing that there were portals on the army base and that a future human had come to visit. He shook his head, bewildered.

Eesha had said she would come on her bike. Ike arrived first and waited at the bicycle racks behind the school. He looked out at the football field and bleachers. Two kids tossed a ball to one another, their shouts distant. He leaned up against the rack and waited. He thought about the map that Mixie had shown them, where they saw the second portal on the base. The sound of bike tires crunching gravel snapped him out of his reverie. Eesha skidded up to him, hitting her brakes at the last minute. She hopped off and placed the front wheel into one of the slots, then leaned on the rack next to Ike.

"So," she started, "your mom's phone played the carnival music?"

"Yeah," Ike answered. "It was coming from her purse."

Eesha shook her head, as if to say, *I knew it all along.*

"She made up some baloney about it being some kind of special military ringtone," Ike went on. "Unbelievable. They both know about it and didn't trust me enough to tell me!"

"So, the military thought they were being secretive using old tech," Eesha said, "sending messages over some kind of special phone. And we just happened to pick up their signal on the old radio."

"Looks that way."

Eesha peered out at the football field, thinking. "What do we do now?"

Ike was taken aback. "I don't know," he said. "I thought you'd have a plan."

She was the one who got them involved in all of this stuff in the first place.

They stood quietly for a moment. The shouts of the kids playing catch sounded in the background.

"What do you want to do, Ike?" Eesha asked in a solemn tone. "She's *your* mom."

Ike thought about that. What *did* he want to do? He knew he wanted his mom to be safe, whatever she was up to. He also wanted to know more about the mission. If there even was one. "I want her to be safe," he said, trying to be as honest as possible. "And I'm mad that they didn't tell me. I deserve to know too, don't I?"

Eesha nodded. "You do, Ike. I'd want to know if one of my parents was going through some kind of . . . time portal. But we don't even know if that's what's really happening. Maybe the army is just studying the portal. We don't have any proof that your mom is going to go through it."

Ike let out a frustrated breath. She was right. They didn't have any proof. But he had a feeling. He just knew it all had to do with his mom.

"Maybe Mixie can help," he said.

"How?"

Ike shifted his weight on the bicycle rack. "Well, if she came back, maybe she could help us get onto the base. See exactly where my mom's going and why."

"I suppose that makes sense."

Ike turned to her. "Let's do it, then. She gave you that . . . card thing. The whatchamacallit?"

"Galactic passport."

"Right. The galactic passport. She said it would tell us what to do."

Eesha slung her pack off her back. "You sure, Ike?"

He nodded.

Eesha fished around in her bag until she found the shiny black card. She set her bag on the ground and held the card up to the sky. "Just looks like a credit card or something."

"Tap it," Ike urged her. "She said to do it twice."

Eesha let out a nervous breath. "Okay. Here goes."

She cradled the galactic passport in the palm of her left hand. With her right index finger, she tapped once in the center and then again.

The card flashed red, then cycled through a myriad of colors, so vibrant they almost had to shield their eyes. Finally, a spinning satellite image of our solar system appeared in the center. A cheerful voice proclaimed: "Mixie's galactic passport, contacting host."

Ike and Eesha looked at each other, speechless.

Small lines of what Ike thought were binary code

scrolled along the bottom edge of the card. Faster and faster they ran, until they were a blur. A *ding* sounded and the satellite image blinked out to reveal a hologram of Mixie's smiling face, pink hair and all.

"What's up, homies!" she exclaimed.

Chapter Twenty-Two

Ike and Eesha quickly ran over to a maintenance area where they were out of sight. They didn't want anyone to see them talking to a floating 3D image.

"I'm glad you guys called," Mixie said. "I told my friends all about you. They're jealous that they didn't come with me!"

Ike noticed a slight delay in Mixie's speech, like when you're watching a show and the actor's mouth doesn't line up with their voice. Out of sync.

"So," Mixie went on. "I got back safely. No trouble at all through the portal. What have you two been doing?"

"Um," Ike began. "I want to know if you can come back. Maybe help us figure some things out?"

Mixie tilted her head curiously.

"Help? How?"

"Well, you know how you said there was another portal on the army base?"

Mixie nodded.

Ike tried to find the right words. What exactly did he want, anyway? He swallowed, fumbling on what to say. Eesha bit her fingernails, and then blurted out: "Ike thinks his mom's going on a mission through that portal and he wants to make sure she's gonna be safe." She said it all in one breath.

Ike closed his eyes and slowly opened them again. "Yeah. What she said."

"So, you really think she is the one to do it? How is she traveling?"

"That's what I don't know," Ike admitted. "But I'm sure of it. I can feel it. I think she's going on a secret mission."

"And the radio message said something about a launch," Eesha added.

"Wow," Mixie said. "You think your mom is going to travel through time? I always read that we didn't do that successfully until the year 2400."

Ike gulped. *Successfully.* That meant there had been people who had tried it and failed! Eesha gave him a sympathetic look.

"You have to help us," he demanded, almost frantic. "She's probably leaving soon. I can tell she's stressed out, but she's trying to hide it. I just need to know she'll be safe!"

Mixie nodded along at Ike's outburst. She was about to speak, but he had more to say. "Maybe you could use your . . . theorem equalizer, or whatever other gadgets you have, to help us get onto the base where my mom works, so I can find out what the mission is about."

Mixie tapped her cheek with a finger, considering. "Well," she finally said. "That's certainly tempting. I wouldn't mind seeing this . . . army base, and if I can help your mom . . ."

Eesha nodded along. She looked at Mixie hopefully.

Ike's heart hammered in his chest.

"Okay!" Mixie shouted. "I'd be happy to help. I just have to sneak away again. My parents have a conference on Kepler-62f tomorrow. Maybe I can do it then."

"We need to do it soon," Ike said.

"I'll come tomorrow," Mixie promised him. "I'll meet you at the portal where I first saw you."

Ike shuddered. "The cement mixer? We can't meet you there! That's where those creeps almost found us before!"

"Yeah," Eesha added. "There has to be another . . . wait. Just come to my house. My dad thinks you're one of my new friends. Which, um, you kind of are."

Mixie smiled. "Sure. I'll see you tomorrow at . . ." She pursed her lips, thinking. "1300 hours."

"Perfect," Ike said. "One o'clock."

"Maximum," Mixie said. "I can't *wait* to see some of your old-school technology."

Ike had to chuckle at that. The base had the most advanced equipment the military had to offer, but to Mixie, it was ancient tech. Like an abacus or something.

"Wish me luck. And not to get stuck," she added.

"Good luck," Ike said.

He thought of the story of Poor Nico and hoped Mixie didn't suffer the same fate. The galactic passport winked out in Eesha's palm.

Ike and Eesha turned to look at one another.

"You ready to do this?" she asked.

"One hundred percent."

Chapter Twenty-Three

There was no going back.

Ike and Eesha were in it up to their necks now. Sneaking onto the army base was definitely illegal. Ike still didn't have any idea how they would do it. *Maybe Mixie can use her theorem equalizer again to help us*, he told himself, as if that made it any less risky.

He met up with Eesha the next day at 12:30. He wanted to get there early to talk about their plans. She met him at the door but stepped outside to join him.

"Needed to get some air," she said. "Sitting in my room staring at the walls isn't helping."

Ike nodded. He'd more or less done the same thing and was pretty wiped out himself.

Eesha checked her watch. "She should be here soon."

They walked around to the back of the house and sat across from each other at the picnic table. The twins crashed through the door and immediately started chasing each other.

"What do you think it all means?" Ike asked. "Everything that's been happening? How does it all fit together?"

Eesha drummed her fingers on the table. "Some kind of mission. But to where or when I don't know."

"It has to be to Mixie's . . . timeline."

"Oh, right," Eesha replied. "She did say something about that."

They sat quietly for a moment. Ike raised his head up to the sun and closed his eyes. The heat usually made him feel awful, but the bright rays on his face felt good for once. The twins' shouts and laughter rang in his ears.

"Are we really doing this?" Eesha asked.

"What?" Ike replied.

"Sneaking onto the base. What if we get caught?"

Ike snorted. "You're the one who suggested it a long time ago. Remember? When we first met?"

Eesha nodded. "I know, but this is—"

"Hello!"

Ike jumped. Mixie walked up to the table. She wore the same type of jumpsuit as she had before, but this one was lavender. And she carried a circular bag by a handle. Ike thought it looked like some kind of high-tech purse. She sat down and placed it on the table. Jack and Jill rushed over and ran in circles around her. Mixie spun around, caught up in their little game. After thirty seconds, they took off again, back to digging holes in the yard or whatever they were doing.

Mixie let out a breath. "Well. Here I am!"

☆ ☆ ☆

With the twins planted in front of the TV in the living room, Eesha led Mixie and Ike down into the basement. Ike was happy to see Mixie again. She didn't seem like an ordinary kid. She was from the future, of course, but she also seemed wiser than anyone he knew. He realized he'd never asked her how old she was. They took seats around the small table.

"Okay," she said, her voice serious. "I can help with whatever you want, as long as I don't do anything here in your timeline to change the future."

Ike and Eesha looked at each other, nervous energy bouncing between them.

Mixie opened her circular bag. Inside, nestled in what looked like black velvet, were several objects, all sleek and silvery.

"Wow," Ike said. "What's all this?"

Mixie pulled out one of the items. It was a small metallic case. She pressed a little hinge and it opened. Inside was a small flashlight.

"A flashlight?" Ike scoffed. "I can use my phone for that."

He looked to Eesha for support, but Eesha was still focused on the object.

"Not a flashlight," Mixie declared.

"Well, what is it, then?" Ike pressed her.

"It's called an inviso-meter. Watch."

Mixie pressed a black button on the side of the device. A thin beam of light slowly streamed from the tip of it. "Who wants to go first?" she asked.

Ike swallowed. He had no idea what this inviso-meter could do, and Mixie seemed to be enjoying keeping them in the dark.

"Me," Eesha offered.

Mixie smiled. "Okay. Very brave. So, just hold out your arm."

Eesha did as she was told.

Mixie waved the device over Eesha's arm. A fine, white mist settled on Eesha's skin. A moment later her arm disappeared.

Ike actually screamed. Eesha gasped and jumped back.

"My arm!" Eesha shouted, panic setting in. "What the . . . ?"

"What did you . . . ?" Ike fumbled. "How did you . . . ?"

"Stay calm," Mixie said in a reassuring tone. "It creates the *appearance* of invisibility. Your arm is still there, of course."

"Unbelievable," Ike whispered.

"Okay," Eesha said. "Um, how do I get my arm back?"

"Easy," Mixie said.

She switched another button on the inviso-meter, releasing another stream of mist, but this one was red. As she waved it where Eesha's arm should have been, it slowly reappeared, knitting itself together. Eesha rubbed her arm. "That . . . is just too weird."

"It kind of freaks me out," Ike said.

"The mist is a type of meta-material," Mixie explained. "It bends light, so the viewer doesn't see the full spectrum of an object."

Ike was trying to wrap his head around the science of it but having a hard time. "So, basically," he said, "it makes you invisible."

Mixie smiled.

"*Maximum*," Eesha whispered.

Ike shook his head in disbelief. "What are you doing with this . . . inviso-meter, anyway? I mean, do you always walk around with it?"

Mixie laughed. "Back home, my friends and I play inviso-tag. The only way to find each other is by our voices. I just happened to have it with me, so . . ."

"So that's how we get on the base?" Eesha asked, still looking at her arm suspiciously. "By going invisible?"

"Probably the best way," Mixie said matter-of-factly.

Ike was still in shock.

They had a decision to make. Ike and Eesha were ready to head to the base, but Eesha was supposed to be watching the twins. There was no way she could leave them. If she did, her mom said she would be on The List, that ominous threat that she really knew nothing about. But it was still scary. She bit her fingernails.

"We can't wait," Ike said, growing agitated. "We have to go now!"

"I know!" Eesha snapped back. "I'm thinking!"

Mixie picked up a Rubik's Cube from the bookshelf and solved it in about twelve seconds.

Eesha stood up and began to pace. "There's only one thing to do," she said.

Ike and Mixie waited in silence.

"I have to take the twins with us."

Ike groaned. "What? Are you sure?"

"Yes," Eesha replied. "I'll just have to keep an eye on them." She turned to Mixie. "That inviso-meter thing. Will it work on the kids?"

Mixie looked up. She placed the Rubik's Cube back on the shelf. "The little ones?" she asked.

Eesha nodded.

"Sure. They're small. Less mass."

Ike shook his head at the strangeness of it all.

"Mixie?" Eesha started. "There isn't anything, uh . . . dangerous about this, is there? I mean, like, for the kids? Are there any kind of . . . side effects?"

Ike thought it was a good question.

"Oh, no," Mixie said casually. "Before the technology was perfected, a lot of people disappeared permanently. But that's all been worked out. Don't even worry about it!"

Ike looked at Eesha. No words needed to be said.

Ike followed Eesha and Mixie up the stairs to the living room. Jack and Jill sat in front of the TV, a bag of chips between them. "Hey, nerd-bots," Eesha called. "C'mon. We're going on an adventure."

Chapter Twenty-Four

The twins tagged along happily, grateful to be out of the house. Ike wasn't exactly sure how they were going to do all of this. If they did get onto the army base, how would he even know where to look for . . . whatever he was searching for?

They walked slowly, each one of them seemingly preoccupied with their own thoughts. Except for the kids, who thought it was all a fun little walk. Ike couldn't focus on any one thing. His mind was racing.

As they continued on, he saw the main gate in the distance, with cars stopping so drivers could show identification to the guards.

"How are we gonna do this?" Eesha asked. "You can't get past the gate without an ID, Mixie."

They all paused. Not many people were around. A few joggers and bicyclists passed them by without even looking their way.

"Okay," Mixie started. "It's time for a little camouflage."

She reached for her round case.

"Wait," Ike warned her. "We need someplace more private." He looked left and then right. "Over there. Behind the pool."

"Good idea," Eesha put in.

The small group followed Ike as he led them to the pool. Fortunately, there were only a few kids and adults standing around as they made their way behind the white brick building. The smell of chlorine hung heavy in the air. "Okay," he said. "This is good right here."

Eesha took a quick look around and pulled the kids closer. Mixie reached into her case and took out the invisometer.

"Who's first?" Mixie asked.

Ike sucked in a breath. "Me."

Eesha shot him a raised eyebrow.

"Okay," Mixie replied. "We'll still be able to hear each other, but we're going to have to be very quiet not to draw attention."

"Got it," Ike said.

"Let's . . . do this," Eesha added.

Eesha turned to the twins, bending down, hands on her knees. "We're gonna play a little game, okay?"

"Yay!" the twins replied in unison.

"But you have to be very, very quiet. Understood?"

She rose back up and faced Mixie. "You're sure about this, right? Nothing will happen to them?"

"I'm sure," Mixie said. "The tech has been around for generations."

Eesha inhaled a deep breath.

And Mixie began her work.

A few minutes later, Ike stood near his friends, guided by the sound of their voices.

"Ike needs to be in front since he knows where he's going," Mixie said. "We'll have to form a chain and hold hands."

"I'll hold on to both of these two," Eesha said. "No way can I let them go."

"We're in-bisible!" Jack said gleefully.

"We can play hide-and-seek!" Jill put in.

"Not now," Eesha warned them. "You two just grab one of my hands. I'm right here. Stick out your arm. It's a game, okay?"

Ike watched, well, nothing. Their voices and shuffling sounds were the only sign that someone was there.

After a few more minutes, they were ready. Mixie had also sprayed her bag with the inviso-meter. They couldn't have a purse floating down the sidewalk.

Ike didn't feel any different, but the reality that he was invisible was certainly unsettling. If INSCOM had this tech, they'd be ecstatic. *Well,* he reconsidered. *They'd probably use it for war.*

They walked quietly. Not speaking. Fortunately, there weren't too many people on the street. But just to be sure, they walked along lawns to avoid bicyclists and joggers. No one would be able to see them, after all.

Ike thought about what they were doing. The main gate wasn't too far. *Are we really going to do this?* he asked himself. *Too late now. We're almost there.*

As they approached, Ike began to sweat. It was a weird sensation. It felt different somehow. He looked down at his invisible feet, leaving soft impressions on the sprinkler-soaked lawn they were crossing. He knew that he, Eesha, and the twins could have gotten onto the base with their IDs. But using the inviso-meter after they entered would be risky.

"Almost there," Eesha's disembodied voice whispered.

"Everyone stay quiet," Mixie warned them. "They won't see us, but they can hear us if we're too loud."

Eesha gave one last warning to the twins, and then they approached the gate.

A military police officer stood there, waving in cars. Ike thought she looked about his mom's age. She wore sunglasses, a white helmet, flak jacket, and camouflage fatigues. Her boots were shined a glossy black. Some kind of gun was strapped in a holster at her side. Ike hated guns. He never even played with toy guns when he was little.

They had to do this quickly before the kids started talking. "Follow me," he whispered.

Instead of getting near the approaching cars, Ike led them around the far edge of the gate by a barbed-wire fence. He felt a bead of sweat on his nose and wiped it away. Slowly, he moved forward, holding on to Mixie's hand behind him. Ten slow seconds passed, and then they were on the other side.

"Unbelievable," he whispered. For a moment, he expected to hear shouts and alarms, but there was no sound except for the '80s soul music from the guard's radio.

"Right," Mixie said softly. "Where to?"

Ike tried to remember what his mom had told him when he'd asked her what she did on the army base. He racked his brain and finally recalled what she had said: *Strategic initiatives.* Also, *intelligence systems and threat identification.*

But there wouldn't be signs for that if it was a secret operation, he realized. He watched the military men and women go about their business as he and the others walked past them. He could literally feel his friends' tension like a presence. Even though he knew people couldn't see him, he still moved warily, as if at any moment he would suddenly become visible again. He couldn't imagine the scandal that would play out if that happened. They'd all be thrown in a military jail for questioning.

"This is fascinating," Mixie's voice chimed behind Ike. They passed an airfield where C-5 cargo planes and others were parked. "These flying craft are so . . . ancient!"

Ike had to chuckle at that.

A small voice sounded behind him, near Eesha.

"Stop touching me!"

"You touched me first!"

"Shh!" Eesha whispered. "Stay quiet. It's a game, remember?"

The twins seemed to be getting bored of the adventure. They had no idea how bizarre the whole escapade was.

"Ike?" Eesha urged. "Where to?"

Ike glanced around in confusion. All of the buildings looked the same—boxlike shapes in beige, gray, or white, and all windowless. Large warning signs were posted at their entrances:

NO ADMISSION.
DEADLY FORCE AUTHORIZED.
WARNING, RESTRICTED AREA.
PHOTOGRAPHY PROHIBITED.

Some of them had letters and numbers that only those in the know could decipher: EED9, RSIT, ISTI. Ike once again thought of turning right back around. But he didn't. This was something he just had to do.

"Wait a minute," he said, looking at a nondescript white brick building with the letter K in bold black lettering. He turned to the building opposite, this one marked with an S.

And then it dawned on him.

"That's it," he said.

"What?" Eesha asked.

"K," Ike said, "as in Kilo. And over there, S, as in Sierra."

Ike couldn't see her, but he was sure Eesha was smiling. "Report Kilo and report Sierra," she said. Ike could hear the excitement in her voice. "*Report* as in *report* to the principal's office. Report to K and S!"

"Right," Ike exclaimed.

"Well, that makes sense," came Mixie's voice.

Walking as quietly as they could, they approached the building marked with a K. The door looked as thick and heavy as solid iron. A gray box with peeling white paint was positioned to the right of it beneath a blinking red light.

"We need some kind of keycard," Eesha whispered.

"Maybe not," Mixie put in. "Good thing I brought my bag."

Ike realized she still had her round case, made invisible by the inviso-meter. He heard the click of a latch opening and then rustling.

"What are we doing?" Jill chirped.

"Shh," Eesha whispered.

"This should work," Mixie said.

A loud buzz followed by a heavy click rang out, and the door opened silently.

"Quickly!" Mixie said. "Stay together. Hold hands."

They all tightened their grips and stepped inside.

"All here?" Ike whispered.

"Yes," Eesha said quietly. "I've got the twins."

Ike peered around. It wasn't a beehive of activity. There were only a few people with headsets hunched over metal desks and staring at computer screens.

Ike needed information on the mission, Quicksilver, or whatever it was called. This place looked to be a mission-control type of area.

"Oh my god," Eesha whispered behind him.

Ike turned to see a giant monitor, and on it was the image of a vehicle. Or some kind of ship. It was gleaming white and didn't look like any military plane or rocket he had ever seen before. It was more like a giant capsule, like a Tic Tac breath mint lying horizontal with windows running along the sides. The word "Quicksilver" was printed in big, black letters on the hull, or whatever the area was called.

"That's it," Ike said quietly. "*Quicksilver!*"

"Wow. That's an odd ship," Mixie said. "I didn't know you had the technology for that yet."

A hissing sound drew Ike's attention away from the video. A door opened on the far side of the room. It wasn't an ordinary door. It was like the ones you see in sci-fi movies that slide open at the push of a button. But that was not what made Ike gasp.

It was his mom, stepping into the room and taking off a futuristic-looking helmet.

"Is that . . . ?" Eesha whispered.

"Yup."

His pulse raced. This all felt too weird, like eavesdropping of the worst kind. They were at his mom's workplace and snooping around right in front of her!

"How's it looking, Pressure?"

Ike turned to the sound of the voice.

It was an older man with gray hair at the temples and horn-rimmed glasses. His army shirt was pressed as stiff as a board and covered in colorful stripes and medals. *Fruit salad,* Ike's dad once called it, which Ike thought was funny. But there was one ingredient in the fruit salad that stood out. A badge for INSCOM, the same one he'd seen at the Fourth of July celebration: United States Army Intelligence and Security Command.

Ike's mom ran a hand through her short hair. "It's looking good, General Davis. Need to focus a bit more on the portal. It's still sending out pulse waves like it did on the Fourth. We need to keep an eye on those."

General Davis nodded, his face as hard as rock. "Fireworks could've interrupted the anomaly and opened up the portal. Last thing the army needs is a civilian stumbling into it. I told the brass they needed to postpone that gosh darn celebration."

"So that's why they canceled the fireworks," Ike whispered.

"And we knew there was something weird about it!" Eesha agreed.

"Are you ready, Pressure?" the general asked.

Ike felt a tightness in his chest. She was really going on the mission! His mom! All of his and Eesha's suspicions were true!

"Affirmative, General," Ike's mom replied. "I've run a

stat check on the space-time anomaly vehicle. Everything is A-OK."

Space-time anomaly vehicle, Ike thought. *That's it. STAV!*

They fell silent for a moment. Ike thought he could hear his own heartbeat.

"Unbelievable," the general finally said wistfully, looking at the ship on the big monitor, "that we live in a time where we can travel to the future and ask for help."

"It's amazing, sir," Natalie said. "And if we get the help we need, we can save the Earth from an inevitable collapse. An end to global warming and climate crisis. All the answers could be waiting for us, right through that portal."

Ike sniffed, and hoped he wasn't overheard. His mom was going on a mission to help the future of Earth. Pride flooded through him. And a gnawing sense of fear.

Ike saw his mother smile, but he thought he saw something else in her eyes, too: fear.

"I want you to go home and get some rest," General Davis ordered her. "What you and your team are doing is a great service to the nation, with significant mortal risk." He paused. "Go and spend some time with your family, Pressure. We'll be shutting down until go time."

Ike froze.

. . . significant mortal risk.

His eyes began to blur and sting. *Don't cry, you idiot!* he screamed in his head. *Not here!*

He watched as his mother brought her right hand up to her brow to give a snappy salute. She turned on her heel and quickly left the room. But not before stopping once in her tracks and looking left and then right.

"What is it, Specialist Pressure?" the general asked.

Ike could hear the twins breathing. They were going to say something.

"I wanna go home!"

Ike almost passed out. His ears rang.

Natalie Pressure whipped her head left and then right. "Who said that?"

"What?" General Davis asked.

"I heard a voice. A child's muffled voice."

Ike squeezed his eyes shut, as if that would help prevent his mom from seeing them. If they were found out, how would he explain what they were doing here? And what would happen? It would be a major security breach. He could see the headline on CNN now:

FUTURE ALIEN SMUGGLED INTO
TOP SECRET ARMY BASE
MILITARY KIDS TAKEN INTO CUSTODY

Ike felt the blood thrumming in his veins.

"Probably just nerves, Pressure," the general offered. "Get some rest. Okay?"

Ike's mom released a heavy sigh but still looked around warily. "Yes, sir. I guess I am a bit tired." She glanced around once more. Ike was only three feet away. Finally, she headed toward the exit.

Only then did Ike Pressure allow himself to breathe again.

Chapter Twenty-Five

Back at Eesha's house, they all gathered in the basement: Ike and Eesha sat across from each other at the table while Mixie took the beanbag. The twins were wiped out from the adventure, so Eesha had an easy time getting them to chill in front of the TV upstairs. The nachos and popcorn certainly helped. She'd told them it was all make-believe, and wasn't worried. If they told their parents that they had turned invisible and gone onto the army base, their parents wouldn't believe them, anyway.

Ike could hardly believe everything he'd seen and heard himself. His mom was going to travel through time! And it seemed like she was doing it alone. "I want to go through the portal!" he said, his mind still spinning. "Maybe I can go through the one in the woods. Where Mixie came through." He pushed his glasses up on his nose. "If I can get there first, maybe I can find a way to protect her from danger."

"And how do you suppose you're gonna do that?" Eesha challenged him. "With your muscles?"

"I don't know," he said softly. "But I'm not gonna stay here and do nothing."

Eesha shook her head. "We don't even know your mom's destination. What if you went through and ended up back in time . . . with giant dinosaurs?"

"That wouldn't happen," Mixie said. She looked like a little kid, sunk down in the orange beanbag. "Remember what I told you about twin portals? They're all part of a . . . chain, I guess you could call it. Kind of like the same highway."

Ike marveled at the science of it all, even though he didn't fully understand it. A thought occurred to him. "Could you, like, travel to any time and place? To see dinosaurs and stuff?"

Mixie rubbed her chin. "Technically, yes. But it would be very dangerous. The further back you travel, the greater the chance of failure. Some people say they've done it, but I don't know if I believe them."

If given the chance, Ike mused, where would he go? He'd definitely want to see dinosaurs. Ancient Egypt and the pyramids. Africa.

"We have to go tonight," he said. "The mission is tomorrow."

Eesha exhaled heavily.

"You heard that general," Ike went on. "He said *significant mortal risk*. I'm not going to let my mom go off alone like that, not knowing what will happen."

"They want to get help for the planet," Eesha said. She looked to Mixie. "Do you think that's something the people in the future would help with?"

Mixie looked doubtful. "I . . . I really don't know what the reaction will be. I don't think I've ever heard of a time traveler from your past coming to our future."

"Will they . . . take her prisoner or something like that?" Ike asked.

"I doubt it," Mixie replied. "My world is pretty peaceful."

"What's it like?" Eesha asked eagerly. "Your world? Our future."

Mixie bit her lip. "I think it's best for you to discover it for yourself. I can take you, Ike."

Ike turned to look at her.

"I understand how you feel. If I can help you get to my time, I will."

Eesha looked at both of them. "We're really doing this? Traveling to the future?"

"I am," Ike declared.

Eesha gave a half grin. "Well, you're not going without me."

"Wait a minute," Ike said. "If we do this, how do we get back?"

"By another portal, of course," Mixie declared.

"But what about time?" Ike went on. "In sci-fi books, sometimes they come back and no time has passed at all. Or very little."

Mixie cocked her head. "Very curious. That's true, for the most part. Time travel is a curved field. A loop, of sorts. It should be fine."

Eesha gulped. "If my parents think I'm missing, they'll call the police or something."

"My dad, too," Ike said.

"We'll work it out," Mixie said, seemingly unconcerned.

Ike and Eesha looked at each other. Eesha seemed to be as freaked out as Ike was.

Mixie stood up from the beanbag. "We're decided, then. I'm taking you to future Earth!"

☆ ☆ ☆

There was no time for goodbyes. Eesha hugged Jack and Jill and told them to stay out of trouble before she left. Ike could tell it wasn't easy, though. She knew that she'd be in a lot of trouble when her parents got home and found them alone. "I have to," she'd said to Mixie. "For Ike, and his mom."

Ike saw her eyes water a little, but he didn't say anything. For a moment, he thought he should run home and see his mom and dad one last time. But he didn't. He might chicken out and confess everything. No, this was something he *had* to do. *Now.*

Ike led them through the woods and kept his eyes peeled for any signs of the mysterious agents. It was getting to be late afternoon, and a few dark clouds scudded across the sky.

"Have you ever heard of Men in Black?" Eesha asked Mixie.

"No. Who are they?"

Eesha reminded her of the goons in the woods, and what she'd discovered about them on the internet.

"Never heard of them," Mixie said.

They walked in silence for a few minutes. Ike's head was pounding. *I'm going to the future. What's going to happen to Mom?*

"Your mother is very brave for going through a portal," Mixie said, as if reading his thoughts.

Ike reflected on that for a moment. "Yes. I think you're right. She is brave. But I wish she'd told me about it."

"She probably didn't want to worry you," Eesha said.

Ike had no reply to that. Either way, he'd still be worried.

He grew quiet. Mixie and Eesha followed, talking softly to one another. It was like everyone was walking on eggshells. Ike was preoccupied with his own thoughts. *Why didn't she ever tell me? Did she tell Dad?*

Several minutes later, they were walking along the trail that led to the cement mixer. Ike's heart hammered in his chest. He didn't want to run into those creeps again, but this was where Mixie said they should go through.

Mixie paused and looked around often. She picked up rocks, tilted her head curiously at the sounds of squirrels and birds.

"Where did you come through, Mixie?" Eesha asked as the cement mixer came into view.

Mixie took out her theorem equalizer and walked between two trees with gnarled and bent branches. The lower branches formed a sort of hoop. It almost looked like a hole, a missing puzzle piece. She began to wave the device around the area until it suddenly turned green. "Here it is," she announced. "You can only find it if you have the right settings."

"Amazing," Eesha whispered, as she and Ike drew closer.

"Wait a minute," Ike said, pointing to the ground below their feet. "Look."

Eesha and Mixie huddled around.

"More footprints," Eesha said.

"Footprints?" Mixie echoed.

"Yeah," Ike said. "I keep finding these. They don't look like . . . a human footprint."

Mixie knelt down to take a closer look. "Some kind of animal?" she ventured.

"We don't know," Eesha said.

"Well," Mixie said, rising back up. "No time to figure it out now. We need to get going."

Ike felt a raindrop on his nose. The wind was picking up, and the tree branches above him swayed and groaned. "Hey," he said to Eesha. "They're going to send Mom through the other portal, right? On the base. The one we saw in Mixie's theorem equalizer."

"True," Eesha said.

"They must not know about the one here, then," Ike went on. "The military. If they did, it would be guarded."

Eesha narrowed her eyes, thinking. "But you know who *does* know something's here?"

"Men in Black," Ike said. "What are they? *Who* are they?"

"Almost ready," Mixie said.

Ike and Eesha turned to look at her.

"So, we just walk through?" Eesha asked.

"We need an energy field first," Mixie explained.

Ike wasn't even going to ask what it was. He was too nervous.

As Mixie fiddled with her device, Ike turned to Eesha. "You're sure you want to do this?"

"Of course!" she exclaimed without hesitation. "We didn't come all this way for me to walk out now, did we?"

Ike smiled. "No. We didn't. I'm glad you're coming."

"Let's just hope Mixie knows what she's doing," Eesha whispered.

"Okay!" Mixie announced.

Ike stared at the space between the trees. The air within it seemed to shimmer. Ike saw little gold specks floating inside of it. "Wow," he whispered.

"We just . . . walk in?" Eesha asked.

"Yes," Mixie said. "Follow right behind me. Whatever happens, keep walking through. Don't turn back. You might find half of you left behind."

Ike waited for Mixie to laugh at her own joke.

She didn't.

Ike and Eesha both took deep breaths.

And then they followed Mixie into the future.

Chapter Twenty-Six

Colors danced at the edge of Ike's vision. A whooshing sound rang in his ears. His head felt as if it were made of Jell-O, like those pictures of a pilot's face distorted by g-forces. He willed his lips to move, but they felt like rubber. "Eesha!" he shouted.

But there was no reply. Only rushing air. Mixie had told him to keep walking forward. It was like pushing through a spongy wall, soft yet firm, his arms outstretched like a hungry zombie.

He closed his eyes and prayed that he would be okay. Beads of sweat popped on his forehead. His pulse raced. He didn't have the strength to wipe it away. His arms felt as if they weighed a thousand pounds.

Hours seemed to pass. He felt as if his body had been left behind and it was just his consciousness traveling. Alone. Forgotten. For a moment, he thought he saw stars and planets swirling in a dark sky.

Finally, time seemed to slow. He opened his eyes . . .

And flew headfirst out of the tunnel as if being shot from a cannon.

Fortunately, he landed on soft ground. He immediately unfolded himself and tried to stand up, but his legs were wobbly and he collapsed.

Eesha came out next, a tumble of arms and legs. "Oof!" she cried.

Ike stood up to see a ring of white light suddenly disappear right where they'd come through.

"I guess we made it," he said, adjusting his glasses. He stretched and looked down at his feet. "Seems like we're all in one piece."

"Yeah," Eesha put in, stretching her neck from side to side. "My head is pounding, though."

"Hey," Ike said, peering around. "Where's Mix—?"

"Over here," Mixie called.

Ike and Eesha turned to see Mixie approaching from their left, looking none the worse for wear. "I came through first," she reminded them.

It took a moment for them to gather their wits. Ike finally took in his surroundings. He had been so disoriented from their journey that he hadn't really looked around yet. They were in a dense green forest, with tall pine trees that soared to a cloudless blue sky. Birds wheeled in the distance. A clean dirt path wound its way along the forest floor. "So, this is it. We're in the future!"

"Let me show you around," Mixie told them.

Ike and Eesha followed Mixie as she led them out of the forest. The flora and fauna seemed the same in Mixie's time as it did in Ike's. But everything was greener and much more vibrant. The leaves on the trees almost looked iridescent. Even the dirt path they walked on seemed to be made up of tiny grains of colorful sand. Ike was reminded of the Zen garden he once had where he would take a little miniature rake and calmly make patterns in the sand.

As they came to the end of the dirt path, the forest and trees grew thin. Ike looked ahead of him in awe.

Everything he had ever imagined about the future could not match this moment. Tall structures soared to the heavens to become lost in the clouds. Some were pyramids made all of glass. Some looked as thin as long needles. Others were like an ocean wave just before it breaks. Aerial ships hovered and zipped across the sky. Not just one, but hundreds, flying in orderly formation. They were all shapes and sizes—round, oval, hexagonal; some with windows and some without. One looked like a black cube within a sphere. Ike saw no signs of propulsion like he did with military planes—no contrails, engine noise, or plumes of smoke. They were silent. He wondered where the stop signs were.

They followed Mixie along a very wide street. The air was fresh and clean. The grass under their feet was soft and spongy. The scent of what he thought was lavender floated on the air. Not a shred of litter could be seen. No cigarette butts. No plastic food wrappers. No empty soda cans or water bottles. And, much to his delight, no giant SUVs driving around like they owned the planet. People of all races passed by, most with a friendly smile or a hello. Quite a few of them wore the same type of jumpsuit as Mixie's. Ike wondered if it was some official uniform or just a fashion choice. Oddest of all, it was quiet. No car horns or music blasting from radios. Ike shook his head in wonder. "This is . . ."

"Amazing," Eesha finished for him.

Eesha halted as a humanoid figure appeared on the path ahead of them. It didn't seem to be walking. It was more like . . . floating, drifting along about five inches from the ground. "Uh," she started, "who or what is *that*?"

"Citi-guides," Mixie explained. "They're artificial intelligence bots. They help tourists and anyone with a question. Watch."

Mixie held up a hand in greeting. The AI bot stopped in its tracks. Ike looked at its face. If not for the glowing green eyes, he would have thought he was looking at a fellow human being. But on closer inspection, the arms and legs seemed just a little too long, giving it an uncanny valley appearance. "Hello," it spoke in a soft voice. "Welcome to New Glades. How may I help you today?"

"Hmm," Mixie started. "We're looking for a good restaurant. Can you recommend one?"

"Searching," the bot replied.

The AI bot began to blink rapidly, its green eyes odd and a little unsettling. After a moment, it suggested several restaurants and gave descriptions of their menus. A holographic image of a menu appeared above the bot's head, and Mixie plucked it from the air.

"That's so cool!" Eesha said.

"It is quite clever, isn't it?" she replied.

"Let me hold it," Ike demanded, eager as a little kid asking for a toy.

Mixie handed it to him, and he turned it over in his hands. It felt like a very thin tablet, smooth to the touch. Ike pressed one of the menu items, and a small hologram popped up showing the entrée in 3D.

"Is there anything else I can help you with?" the bot went on. "There is a special on solo flights to Phobos and Deimos. Only four hundred credits per passenger. Children ride for half-price."

Mixie laughed. "No. But thank you for letting us know."

Ike's mouth fell open. "Phobos? Deimos? That's . . . Mars, right?"

"Yup," Mixie replied. "Didn't I tell you Mars was colonized in 2057? We can go if we have time."

Ike was too shocked to reply. To his surprise, the hologram menu winked out and disappeared from his hands. The AI bot continued to blink, its green eyes bright in the sun.

"Let me ask it something." Eesha drew a little closer. "Okay, um. Will the Detroit Lions ever win a Super Bowl?"

Ike rolled his eyes. "All of the information in the world at her fingertips and she asks about . . . sports."

The bot blinked rapidly. "I am sorry. The answer is . . . no."

Eesha shrugged.

Mixie led them to an area in the center of the city called the Quad, with wide streets bordered by massive trees. Instead of billboards, like those on a highway, on either side of the boulevard, several large screens hovered in midair, showing images of some kind of sporting event. Two opposing teams zipped around on what looked like unicycles chasing a small golden globe. On another, a band of musicians in costumes that seemed to be made completely of flowers played an assortment of odd instruments

Ike had never seen before. He assumed they were wind instruments, seeing as how the players held them up to their mouths. But the shapes were odd—long and twisted like tubas and saxophones designed by a mad scientist.

People continued to shuffle by, some talking to small holograms in their peripheral vision.

"This looks . . . really cool," Eesha said. "Is all of the world like this city?"

"Only a few places," Mixie replied, a hint of pride in her voice. "This is called New Glades. My home. There hasn't been a war here in over five hundred years."

"What about the government?" Ike ventured. "Politicians? Who runs things?"

Mixie looked at Ike, thoughtful. "The people are as one. We learned long ago to live in peace and govern ourselves."

"Amazing," Eesha said. "A real utopia."

"If this is where my mom's mission is headed, I think she'd be completely safe!" Ike said.

"That general dude said she was coming here to ask for help in our time," Eesha said.

"But how?" Ike asked. "Who does she talk to? If there's no . . . president, how does she get help?"

"There are several organizations that look after the

planet," Mixie explained. "She'll probably want to talk to the Galactic Council."

Galactic Council, Ike mused. A name straight out of a sci-fi novel.

"So," Eesha said in a serious tone. "Ike's mom. We need to find out where she's going to come in. Will it be the same portal we came through?"

"There's someplace I want to show you first," Mixie said.

Ike shot her a side-eye. "Are you sure?"

"We've got time," Mixie said. "It'll be fun! Promise."

Ike and Eesha followed Mixie, although Ike was a little annoyed that they didn't really have a plan yet for finding his mom.

She led them down a street with busy shops on both sides. Every one of them looked like a candy store with flashing lights and holographic displays. One window showed mannequins posing in the same jumpsuits everyone seemed to be wearing. Another window display boasted a silver ship with a sign next to it that read: WARP DRIVE CHARGER. NEW THIS YEAR. ONLY 5,000 CREDITS. Ike pressed his nose up against the window. It was the coolest thing he had ever seen. A wraparound windscreen was in the front, and it sat on three legs like a camera tripod, cocked at an aggressive angle. "Wow," he exclaimed.

Mixie sidled alongside him. "Do you like it?"

Ike backed away from the window. "Uh, yeah."

"C'mon," she urged them. "It's not too far now."

In a matter of a few minutes, they were standing at the entrance of a giant skyscraper. Ike looked through the glass. He gasped. Several small disk-shaped crafts flew around in circles and zigzags. He craned his neck up. He didn't see a roof, just blue sky. "Wow!" he exclaimed again.

They followed Mixie inside, where she made a quick transaction with a teenager who handed her something that looked like a black-and-gold bracelet. She slipped hers on, then turned around and gave one each to Ike and Eesha.

"What are these for?" Ike asked.

"You want to fly one, don't you?"

A smile formed on Ike's face.

"Heck, yeah, we want to," Eesha exclaimed.

"They prevent motion sickness," Mixie said.

Ike felt his stomach churn.

After they'd put on the bracelets, Mixie led them to an area where several of the vehicles were parked. They all had the wraparound windscreens. Ike eyed a sleek silver one. Eesha set her sights on a green one.

"Don't go up too high," Mixie said. "There's an invisible barrier up there you can run into."

"Oh," Ike said, nervously.

"And ships on your left always have the right of way. Remember that and you should be okay!"

Ike was growing more nervous by the second.

"Who wants to race?" Eesha boasted.

"Do you have to be so competitive?" Ike asked. "I just want to fly!"

But as cool as it was, he was a little hesitant. He didn't know how to drive. How hard would it be to steer an aerial ship?

A few minutes later, Mixie helped strap them both in and showed them how to work the controls. It was fairly simple. Ike thought of bumper cars he had driven when he was a kid.

"So," Mixie began, calling to both of them from within her ship, her voice coming from a little screen on the console of Ike's craft. "Go slow to start. And watch the other ships around you. These ships aren't like the real thing, but they're close. It's pretty hard to actually get hurt though."

Ike felt his adrenaline racing.

"So," Mixie went on, "all you have to do is press the little green button right next to the—"

"This one?" Ike replied.

Eesha screamed as Ike shot up into the air.

Ike held on to the small wheel as the craft swayed from side to side. "Whoa!" he shouted from two hundred feet in the air, trying to even it out.

Mixie buzzed up alongside him. Eesha soon followed. Of course, she took to it like a pro right away.

While Mixie and Eesha flew in circles around Ike, making sure he was okay, he finally started to get the hang of it. He looked up into a brilliant blue sky. "This is amazing!" he screamed, as other fliers buzzed around him.

"I know!" Eesha shouted back from her craft.

Ike felt a little disoriented, but not as much as he would have thought. *Must be the bracelet.*

"There's a game they play up here called Float," Mixie said. "It's pretty cool. We should try it!"

Nope, Ike thought immediately.

"Hit the green button again, and you'll drop down like you're in an elevator. It'll automatically stop before you reach the bottom."

"Let's do it!" Eesha screamed.

Ike watched as her craft immediately dropped. He gulped. "Okay. Green button." He reached out with a trembling finger, closed his eyes, and pressed.

His ship dropped at an impossible speed. He opened

his eyes and leaned back in the contoured seat. It was over in seconds, but it felt like minutes. When he reached the bottom, the ship gently swayed for a moment and then quietly settled on the floor.

They all climbed out of their vehicles. Eesha's eyes were wide with excitement. "Let's do it again!"

"I think that was enough for me," Ike admitted, a little woozy now. "We need to find my mom."

"Ike's right," Eesha put in. "We didn't come all this way to—"

Ike jumped as a siren wailed through the city.

Eesha clamped her hands over her ears. They all rushed outside.

"What's happening?" Eesha shouted over the din.

"What the—?" Mixie exclaimed. It was the first time Ike had heard her sound alarmed.

Eesha pointed to one of the many screens lining the streets, all displaying the same image, accompanied by a robotic-like voice:

"Foreign interdimensional craft detected. Possible invasion of unknown origin or species. Please stay calm and seek shelter."

Ike peered at the image on the screen. It was fast-moving—a capsule-like white blur.

"It can't be," Eesha whispered.

Ike narrowed his eyes, studying the image. "That's my mom's ship!" he said, nervous energy beginning to flood his body. "*Quicksilver.* It looks just like the one we saw on that screen at her work!"

The siren wailed even louder. People began to run to their hover cars and flying ships. It wasn't a panic, Ike saw, but close to one.

"We have to get to my house," Mixie said. "I don't know how I'm going to explain you to my dad, but we don't have any other choice! Follow me!"

"What about my mom?" Ike shouted. "It looks like she's gonna be here any minute. We can't just leave!" He began to panic. "Mixie, you have to . . . you have to take me to the police, or the government or whatever. I need to tell them she's not dangerous!"

"Hold on, Ike," Mixie said. "First things first. *Breathe.*"

Ike went silent. He took a deep breath.

"And again," Mixie urged him.

Ike felt a little better, but he was still agitated.

"Okay," Mixie began. "Your mom's ship is nowhere near us yet. We have dimensional radar that picks up anything entering this . . . time and place."

"Okay," Ike said hesitantly.

"And," she went on, "it may have *seemed* like we traveled here in minutes, but actually, it took *hours*. When we travel through time, our cells and DNA have to be shifted and realigned to enter—"

Ike didn't understand it. He knew he'd have to face the music when he got home, but right now, at this moment, he didn't care.

"So when will she be here, then?" he asked Mixie.

Mixie turned to peer at one of the screens. "See that little countdown along the bottom?"

Ike looked. "Yeah."

"Says ninety minutes," Eesha said.

"That's how long it's going to take for her to enter our time continuum," Mixie explained.

"Weird," Eesha whispered.

"So, for now," Mixie said, "let's go to my house and ask my parents for help. My mom will know what to do."

Ike looked to Eesha. "She knows what she's doing, Ike. We have to trust her. We don't know anything about how time works here, right?"

Ike adjusted his glasses. "Right," he relented.

"Follow me," Mixie commanded them.

Ike and Eesha followed Mixie down the street. The siren was still ringing, a piercing, high-pitched warning.

"Here," Mixie said, stopping at a row of ships parked on the side of the boulevard. Ike and Eesha watched as she took her theorem equalizer out of her case and waved it over a matte-black disk-shaped craft. The doors rose and opened from the inside, like wings, and Mixie climbed in. "C'mon, guys. Let's go!"

Ike and Eesha followed, a little awed by their means of transport. Comfortable seats were along one wall, and the front display showed a control panel with blinking multicolored lights, a lot different than the ships they were just flying for fun. This was the real thing. Mixie punched something into the touch screen, and the vehicle lifted up. "Hold on!"

Ike looked for something to grab on to, and the closest thing was Eesha's hand. She squeezed back as he clasped it. He thought they both felt a little weird about it, but they didn't let go until the ship's rapid ascent smoothed out and seemed steady.

As the ship continued to climb up into the sky, Ike looked through the window at the city growing small beneath them.

"How does this thing work?" Eesha asked.

"It's all automated," Mixie explained. "You just have to put in a destination, and it does the rest. I don't even have to steer!"

"Unbelievable," Ike whispered.

"Maximum," Eesha said. She turned to Ike. "They

must have changed the mission date. I thought it was tomorrow!"

"I know," Ike said. "Maybe it's already tomorrow there, if you know what I mean."

The craft began to descend. Ike felt as if his head was going to pop from the pressure. They landed softly, much to his relief, and the winglike doors silently opened and lifted up again.

Ike took a look around as they climbed out. They had landed several feet away from a white dome-like structure, surrounded by topiary in the shapes of animals. Other dome houses dotted the area, some white and others a myriad of colors. It reminded Ike of a botanic garden he once visited. The lawns were so green, he thought they must have been fake.

"Welcome to my home!" Mixie announced.

"Mixie Gold!" a voice shouted as they approached. "Get in here this instant! There's an invasion coming!"

Chapter Twenty-Seven

Mixie Gold, Ike mused. *Cool name.*

They followed Mixie into the dome house. The door silently slid closed behind them. Ike peered around warily. Oddly, it was decorated the way he imagined a house from the 1960s would be. He'd seen pictures and TV shows of that era, and this place seemed very similar, but with a few strange touches. There was a sunken living room area, with little steps leading down to a big white circular couch and cushions. The floor was carpeted in shaggy fluorescent green. A large flat-screen showing tranquil nature scenes floated in the air above what looked like a fireplace. The furniture was white, beige, or cream-colored. Ike didn't see a speck of dust anywhere.

Mixie led them to the living room, where her dad paced back and forth furiously. "It's on all of the alert systems!" he scolded her. "They're telling everyone to stay at home. It could be . . . an invasion of some sort!"

Mixie snorted. "Not so sure about that, Dad. I think it's my friend's mom."

Mr. Gold cocked his head like an inquisitive bird. In fact, that's what he looked like: a very tall bird. All of his features seemed a little exaggerated, especially his ears. His hair went every which way and reminded Ike of a picture he'd seen of Albert Einstein. The long green bathrobe he wore added to his quirkiness.

Mr. Gold glanced at Ike and Eesha as if only now noticing them. "Who are these two . . . children?"

Ike and Eesha traded a glance.

"This is Ike and his friend Eesha," Mixie explained. "They're . . . they're from our past."

Silence.

"Past?" Mr. Gold finally repeated.

Mixie sighed. "Dad. You better sit down."

Mixie brought Ike and Eesha glasses filled with a sweet fruity drink and began talking. Mr. Gold ran a hand through his wild hair and shook his head in disbelief every few seconds. Finally, she finished, and Mr. Gold studied Ike and Eesha suspiciously. "So, you're really from our . . . past?"

Ike and Eesha nodded.

Mr. Gold turned to his daughter, clearly distressed.

"Mixie, you've always been told to stay away from portals and time-travel devices! They should only be used in case of a dire emergency!"

"I'm sorry, but it's too late for that now, Dad. We need to find a way to talk to the Galactic Council. That ship they detected is on a mission. And Ike's mom is flying it!"

"Galactic Council!" Mr. Gold shot back. "And how are we supposed to do that? You can't just send a holo to the Galactic Council."

Ike took a breath. "If I could just meet with them, sir, I could tell them myself. That I'm from the past . . . and that all my mom wants to do is ask your world for help."

Mr. Gold looked at him as if he had never seen a teenage boy before. "Help? What kind of help?"

Ike thought on that a moment. His mom's mission could provide the hope that humankind needed. Now more than ever. "She's on a top secret assignment. She's in the army, and she's under . . . significant mortal risk, coming here to ask for help."

Mr. Gold nodded. "Go on, then."

"Well, sir. Our world is suffering from . . . terrible things. The polar ice caps are melting. The oceans are rising. There are wildfires everywhere. Climate change and global warming are destroying the planet."

Ike caught Eesha's serious expression at the corner of his vision, as she nodded along.

Mixie's dad shook his head. "I . . . don't . . . know. This is—"

"Dad!" Mixie's voice was urgent. "We have to find a way to contact the council. Does Mom know someone high up who will listen to us? Where is she, anyway?"

Mr. Gold looked like he was about to put Mixie on The List.

"She's not here. I cannot believe how foolish you've been, Mix! Using a portal to get to the past, and then bringing your little friends back with you!" He waved his hands around in the air. "They . . . they could have"—he stared at Ike and Eesha in horror—"germs!"

Eesha screwed up her face. "Really? Germs?"

"We haven't had a pandemic in years," Mixie said.

"Doesn't mean it can't happen," her father countered.

Ike could see Eesha was fuming, arms crossed, scowling.

"Dad," Mixie started again. "I'm going to send a holo to Mom. We need to tell the council to, uh . . ."

"To stand down," Ike said.

"Right," Mixie said. "Stand down."

Mr. Gold's face was turning a shade of red Ike had

never seen before. "You are doing no such thing, Mix."

Mixie seemed to be at a loss for words. She bit her lip, obviously thinking on what to do. Ike saw another side of her then, the mischievous side she had mentioned when they'd first met—when he had asked her why she had come through a portal in the first place. Her eyes gleamed for a moment and then—

"Run!" she shouted, and bolted for the door.

Ike and Eesha jumped at the sound of her voice, then froze in surprise.

"C'mon!" she cried out.

"And where do you think you're going?" Mr. Gold bellowed, running after them, his robe flapping around his skinny knees.

"I'm sorry, Dad," Mixie declared. "But I said I would help my friends, and that's what I'm going to do!"

She pressed a button on the wall, and the sliding panel door shot up. Ike felt the cool air on his face as they ran toward the ship that had brought them there. The house was way too warm for his liking. Or maybe it was just his own rising anxiety.

They hopped in, and Mixie pressed a green button on the ship's console. The next thing Ike knew, they were flying again. He looked out of the windscreen. They passed over a giant golden statue of a man cloaked in white with his open palm facing out; some type of outdoor mobile, like the one Ike had above his bed when he was a kid, with revolving balls of various colors moving on their own with no signs of strings or motors; a gleaming octagonal pool of sparkling blue water, ten times as large as the army base's pool. He must have closed his eyes too many times on the way there to notice them.

Mixie touched a small tablet-size screen on the console. Ike saw her image come up like she was making a video call. "Mom. I need to talk with you. It's important. You have friends at the council, right?"

Blurry static appeared on the screen, and then an automated voice sounded throughout the craft:

All communications down. Authorized personnel only. Please enter your security code.

"Great," Mixie said. "Just great."

Ike sighed in desperation.

"We have to get to the Galactic Council!" Mixie shouted, as the ship settled to the ground. "As quickly as possible."

They all climbed out. Ike's head spun. His whole reason for visiting the future was to try to make sure his mom was going to be safe. Now, here he was, and she was still in danger!

"Where is it?" Eesha asked. "This Galactic Council?"

"It's in a highly secure building," Mixie replied. "You need official clearance to get in."

"Great," Eesha said. "Just fantastic."

"I don't know if we can get in, but my mom has friends there, so we can try," Mixie said. "I don't care what my dad says."

Every few minutes, the warning voice would announce once again for citizens to clear out and seek shelter. Ike had no idea where it was coming from, but it seemed like everywhere all at once—to his left, right, and above.

"So, Mixie," Eesha started as they hurried along. "What does your dad do, anyway?"

Mixie let out a snort. "He writes books. A novelist. He's highly strung, if you know what I mean."

"He did seem . . . very distressed," Eesha replied.

"Well," Ike said, "he was worried about you."

"He's always like that," Mixie replied. "My mom calls it his artistic temperament." She paused. "We better get off the street soon. It's getting . . ."

Ike turned around to the sound of heavy footfalls.

Several figures in gleaming, futuristic armor stood behind them.

"Uh-oh," Mixie said, as they all froze.

"What?" Eesha replied, alarmed. "Who are they?"

"Peace Force," Mixie whispered. "A branch of the Galactic Council."

"Halt right there," a voice sounded.

The group approached them cautiously. Ike didn't see any weapons like a police officer would carry, but their armor, if that's what it was, looked like metal, with several small instruments strapped to their chests. A white dove was emblazoned on their helmets.

"Which one of you is Mixie?" one of them asked, a woman with blond hair peeking from beneath her helmet.

Ike gulped.

Mixie raised her hand meekly.

"Thanks for your compliance," the woman said. "Your father reported that you are hiding two fugitive time travelers." She paused and looked at Ike and Eesha. "According to Rule 87654 of the Galactic Council, I'm placing all three of you under arrest."

Chapter Twenty-Eight

Ike, Eesha, and Mixie were sitting in a bare white room with only three metal chairs. A logo with a white dove in flight was painted onto the wall, just like the Peace Force officers' helmets. There weren't any bars, like a prison would have, but they were definitely being detained.

"We've done it now," Ike said.

"Never thought I'd be called a time-traveling fugitive," Eesha moaned.

Ike didn't reply to Eesha's quip. He was nervous and afraid. He had to find a way to communicate with his mom or the council.

"I can't believe my dad did this!" Mixie said. "What in the world was he thinking? We have to get out of here!" She paced back and forth, muttering under her breath.

Eesha chewed a fingernail. Ike turned to her. "What are we gonna do?"

She didn't respond immediately, only stared at the bare

floor. "I don't know, Ike. We had no way to plan for this."

Ike looked at the floor as well. "I know. It's all so . . . unbelievable. But there has to be a way!"

Mixie gasped. "I still have it!" she suddenly burst out.

"What?" Ike asked.

She pulled her theorem equalizer from her pocket. "They didn't search us. Basic human rights and all that. Now I need to see if it can get us out of here."

Ike sighed in relief. He realized he was very tired. It was like some kind of time-travel jet lag. He felt unfocused and a little dazed.

Mixie walked to the far wall where they had been led in through sliding doors, but there was no sign of a crack or seam. She ran her device over the smooth surface like a carpenter searching for studs.

"What are you doing?" Eesha asked.

"There's an opening here. We just can't see it, right?"

"Yes," Ike replied. "That's where we came in. Uh, I think. Maybe a little to the left?"

Mixie slowly moved the device to the left. An electronic hiss sounded and the wall parted.

"Yes!" she whispered.

The open doors revealed an empty hallway. Ike and Eesha stood up to join Mixie.

"I don't know my way around this place," she said quietly, leaning out halfway to look around. "Just try and act normal."

They exited and the doors softly closed behind them. They were in a long white hallway, with dim yellow lights on the ceiling. A glass door was at the very end. They crept along quietly. Somewhere in the distance, Ike heard the high-pitched whine of the siren outside.

"We just have to find an exit," Mixie said softly.

"There can't be much time left before my mom gets here," Ike said. "We have to—"

Footsteps sounded behind them.

"Run!" Mixie shouted.

They all took off, running as fast as they could. They sped around a corner.

Another hallway.

Then another.

The place was like a maze, Ike realized. How would they ever find an exit?

"Halt!" a voice called.

Every instinct was telling Ike to stop and turn around with his hands up, but it didn't look like Mixie or Eesha had the same idea.

"Through here!" Mixie shouted, as they came to the

end of the hall. To the left, Ike saw rays of light at the end of another long passage. They sped toward it, his lungs burning.

"Alert!" a voice cut through the air.

"Alert! Action stations! Action stations! All forces to the Quad! Unknown craft exiting dimensional time portal at sector six."

The rushing footfalls behind them suddenly ceased. Ike risked a look behind him. The Peace Force was retreating! An unidentified "unknown craft" was certainly more important than a few kids getting into trouble. They all paused and bent over, hands on knees, breath coming fast.

"Is that where we came through?" Ike asked, winded. "The dimensional time portal? Sector six?"

"No," Mixie said. "It has to be some other portal than the one we came through from your time."

"We have to get out there!" Ike shouted, rushing toward the door and pushing it open.

They ran into the sunlight.

And stopped dead in their tracks.

Several airships hovered in the sky. Yellow and white orbs floated alongside them. Ike squinted. These ships didn't look like the ones at the flying amusement center or the one that Mixie had flown. They were all deep green and emitted a low hum Ike could feel vibrating in his chest. Other ships, emblazoned with the white dove logo, hovered in the distance.

This was the moment, he realized. He had to save his mom and her ship. "I have an idea."

"What?" Eesha asked.

Ike didn't reply. He turned to Mixie. "Do you still have your . . . galactic passport?"

She tapped the pockets of her jumpsuit. "Passport? Where did I put that—"

"I have it," Eesha said sheepishly, reaching in her pocket. "Forgot to give it back to you."

"No worries," Mixie said, taking it from Eesha and handing it to Ike. "What are you going to do?"

Ike took the card in his hands. "So," he started. "If we were able to reach you across time on this galactic passport, maybe we can reach my mom, too."

Mixie nodded. "Not a bad idea. Here. Give it back a sec."

Ike handed it to her.

She tapped the card a few times. "I set it for all open frequencies," she said, giving it to him again. "Never done that before. It's like an open door for strangers. Kind of like your . . . junk mail?"

Ike understood the analogy well.

He looked up. Red lights on the bottom of the green ships began to pulse. "What does that mean? Are they gearing up for shooting missiles or something?"

Mixie followed his gaze. "I don't know, Ike. I've never seen ships like these before."

The siren started up again. Ike saw that several people had gathered near the Quad. Obviously the instructions to seek shelter were not working. Something big was about to happen, and people wanted to see it. The crowd grew larger every minute, ignoring the calls from the Peace Force officers trying to control the situation.

There was still no sign of Ike's mom's ship.

"Try her now," Mixie said. "If she sees your face instead of mine, she might listen. She doesn't know who I am."

Ike cradled the card in his hand. "Here goes," he said. He looked to Eesha, who nodded in support. Then he let out a breath and tapped the card twice. "Hello . . . this is Ike Pressure, searching for Natalie Pressure. Mom, if you can hear me, please reply! Over."

They waited in silence for a response, static, anything. But nothing came, only more dead air.

Ike's heart fell. There was no way to reach her. How in the world did he expect her to hear him as she was hurtling through time? He remembered how he felt when he came through: disoriented and weak. He couldn't imagine what his mom was feeling. They waited in silence for what seemed an eternity.

"Try it again," Eesha urged him. "You have to keep trying."

The card in Ike's hand flashed red. He gasped as a pixelated image of his mom's face slowly came in to focus.

"Mom!" he shouted, as Eesha and Mixie gathered around.

"Ike?" came the astonished reply.

Chapter Twenty-Nine

Ike couldn't believe what he was looking at. It was his mother, wearing the same helmet he had seen her in at her office on the base. "Mom!" he cried out.

"Ike?" came his mother's voice again, broken up by static and flashes of white. "What in the world?"

"Mom!" he repeated. "You have to be careful! Where are you? They're going to shoot you down!"

The image winked out.

The hair on Ike's arms suddenly stood on end. The earth underneath him trembled, as if a quake was about to split the ground asunder. "What's happening?" he asked.

In answer, Mixie pointed to the heavens.

Ike blinked.

A long tunnel-like hole had opened in the sky. Swirling flashes of red and green burst within its depths. Small drones shot out of the Peace Force ships and zoomed into it.

"It's a portal," Mixie whispered.

Ike couldn't take his eyes off the massive wormhole. It looked like a tornado but lying on its side, horizontal.

"That must be the other end of the portal on the base," Eesha suggested.

"And my mom's ship is gonna come blasting out of there any second!" Ike said, unable to keep the fear and worry out of his voice.

But they were mistaken.

A massive green craft silently lumbered out of the wormhole.

"Is that one of yours?" Eesha asked Mixie.

Mixie's face faded to a ghostly white. "No," she said, shaking her head. "But I've seen pictures of it before."

"Where?" Eesha asked warily.

"In my Intergalactic Studies class. The only enemy to ever invade us. We held them back before, but that was long, long ago."

Ike swallowed. "Who? Who are . . . ?"

The answer was revealed as a hologram took shape in the sky.

Two figures, all in black.

Familiar figures. But it couldn't be. Not here. Not now.

"What in the—?" Eesha started.

It was the same man and woman they had seen at the cement mixer. But now they looked a little different. They seemed out of proportion, their bodies oddly lanky and their clothes too big, as if they were hiding some grotesque shape underneath.

"The Men in Black," Ike whispered.

As if on cue, the figures in the hologram *morphed* to reveal their true shapes. It was like something out of a nightmare. They stood upright, like a human would, but their skin was covered in scales. Yellow vertical-pupil eyes stared out at them. They wore armor on their chests like something out of a medieval fantasy novel. In their hands, they carried broad-edged swords. Ike almost fainted.

"They're not Men in Black," Mixie said flatly, as if she were entranced. "They're Reptilians."

Ike shook his head, flabbergasted. "Reptilians?"

"We are here to claim what is ours," one of them spoke, and the sound came through the unseen speakers around the city. It was like a hissing snake, sibilant and deadly. Ike was reminded of the hiss he'd heard near the cement mixer. How could this be real!

A forked tongue darted from the creature's mouth. "Our race has been here since the beginning of time. We are the true rulers of this world, and now we will claim what is ours!"

The image blinked out as a blue flash erupted from the Reptilian ship. The Peace Force ship dropped low to avoid it, and the blast flew into a glass building, leaving a smoking, gaping hole.

"It's all true," Eesha said quietly. "Aliens. Reptilians..."

"They're a warlike species who believe the universe is theirs and theirs alone," Mixie said. "They only live for conquest."

"The footprints in the forest," Ike said, aghast. "They belonged to these... Reptilians. The Men in Black."

"They're shape-shifters," Eesha added quietly.

"What were they doing on Earth?" Ike asked.

"They must've come here through the portal from your world that was opened!" Mixie said.

Ike turned away from the sky and tapped the galactic passport again. "Mom! Mom! You have to stay back. There's danger here!"

No reply.

But right at that moment, more swirling flashes of red and green burst from within the wormhole's depths and *Quicksilver*, his mother's ship, surged through in a deafening roar.

"That's her!" Ike shouted.

A beam of light shot from one of the Peace Force ships, narrowly missing *Quicksilver*.

"Stop!" Ike shouted, waving his arms. "Don't shoot at

her!" He imagined himself as an ant on the ground, just a tiny speck. "Please stop!"

Another bolt of pure blue lightning shot out of the Reptilian ship, knocking one of the Peace Force's ships out of the sky. Ike watched as it fell to earth in a fiery crash.

"Oh, no," Eesha said. "This is bad."

The Peace Force returned fire on the Reptilian ship, which now turned bright red as a wave of fire and smoke poured forth from it, like a dragon belching fire. Another Peace Force ship crashed to earth.

"Stop!" Ike shouted, his voice sounding small and weak in the midst of all the noise and explosions.

"We have to find some kind of shelter!" Eesha cried out.

Ike knew she was right. He was so caught up in protecting his mom, he wasn't thinking of their own safety.

The crowd that had been watching the spectacle was already gone. But not Ike and his friends. They were not going to give up. "This way!" he called, leading them behind a wall covered in lush green vines.

Suddenly, *Quicksilver* turned and swooped, emitting a blast of yellow fire right into the center of the Reptilian ship.

"Yay!" Ike shouted. "Go, Mom!"

"She has weapons on that thing?" Eesha exclaimed, surprised.

Pride flooded Ike's heart. "I guess they wanted to be safe. Time travel can lead you to some dangerous places."

"Like here," Eesha said.

Another Peace Force ship took aim at the enemy, sending it spinning.

"They're working together!" Mixie said. "They see that your mom isn't firing at them!"

And as Ike watched, he realized it was true. The Peace Force continued to bombard the enemy as *Quicksilver* darted around like a fast-moving Tic Tac, firing sonic blasts and rays.

Finally, the Reptilian ship let out a squealing groan, the loudest sound Ike had ever heard—grinding metal on metal and expanding steel—until it came down in a blazing fireball.

Ike pumped his fist in the air. "That's my mom!" he shouted, his voice breaking. "That's Specialist Natalie Pressure right there!"

Eesha smiled. Ike saw that her eyes were a little glassy. His probably were, too.

"Your mom," Mixie said in awe, "is a badass."

"Another old-school slang term you learned in school?" Eesha asked.

"One hundred percent."

They ran as fast as they could in the direction of the downed ship. Sirens blared and onlookers suddenly appeared again, taking it all in.

"She's got to come down now," Ike said. "She has to land somewhere!"

Quicksilver came down to earth in a soft landing, right in the middle of the Quad. Ike saw no visible signs of propulsion as it settled onto the ground. How did it work?

A troop of Peace Force soldiers rushed to the scene. "Stand back!" they shouted at the excited onlookers. "We don't know what this creature is. It could be contaminated."

"It's not a creature!" Ike shouted. "It's my mom! And she doesn't have any . . . diseases!"

He was glad Eesha and Mixie held their laughter. The situation was much too dire.

A hatch on top of the craft slowly opened with a groan and a creak.

The Peace Force officers raised their weapons. Ike held his breath as his mother's helmeted head rose up. Her gaze landed on her son.

"Ike Pressure! What in the world!"

And then she passed out.

Chapter Thirty

Everything in the Galactic Council chambers was a muted gray, except for the marble floor, which portrayed a scene of doves in flight against a rainbow-colored background. The room was the size of a small auditorium, with a gallery of chairs grouped close together below a raised platform, on which several large high-backed chairs were arranged in a semicircle. A white dove was emblazoned high on the wall behind them, like a presidential seal.

Ike stared at his mom, who was looking straight ahead.

He was seated below the platform with his mom, Eesha, and Mixie, as if they were awaiting trial. It was an intimidating place, the complete opposite of the greenery and sunshine outside. Whoever designed it must have loved Roman and Greek architecture. The Doric and Corinthian columns soared to a roof with diagonal rays of sunlight streaming in. Ike once saw a picture of the Pantheon in Rome, and this ceiling was very similar, with an opening to the sky called an oculus.

On the platform, the leader of the Peace Force, a woman referred to as Peacekeeper Margot, sat flanked by six other people, three on each side of her, all wearing gleaming white robes. Her demeanor was stern, but her eyes held compassion. Two silver braids hung from either side of her face. "So, you came from our past to ask for help?"

"Yes . . . um, Your Honor?" Ike's mom replied.

Peacekeeper Margot almost smiled. "Peacekeeper will do," she said bluntly.

Natalie Pressure nodded. "Yes, Peacekeeper. I did come from my time to ask for your help. But I didn't know my son would be here as well." She turned to Ike. "How did you even know about the mission, Ike? This is serious business."

"You didn't tell me," Ike said, trying his best to defend himself. "So, I had to find out by myself."

"And I helped," Eesha put in.

Ike's mother shot her a withering look. "I wouldn't be so quick to admit that."

Eesha shrunk.

"Those creatures," Natalie went on, turning back to Peacekeeper Margot. "Who are they? What are they?"

Ike had asked himself the same question. Margot leaned back in her chair. "A warlike species called Reptilians. We were in a war with them hundreds of years ago and thought they were defeated. They are the renegades of the galaxy, causing war and destruction wherever they go. The time-warp signature of your ship left a beacon for them to follow."

Time-warp signature? Ike thought, dumbfounded.

"I noticed them as I went through the space-time anomaly," Natalie Pressure said softly, as if talking to herself. "I knew something was tailing me, but I didn't know what."

"If your son hadn't used the galactic passport to hail you, you would have never known to fire on that enemy ship. Our weapons are not as . . . deadly as our ancestors'." Peacekeeper Margot's lips made a severe thin line. "We do not approve of your weapons of death, Pressure. But you helped us prevent a war of galactic proportions. Most likely, that first ship was only a scout, with others waiting in the wings. Now they will reconsider. Let's just hope they don't try to attack again."

Ike raised his hand tentatively, as if he were in the principal's office for acting out.

Peacekeeper Margot nodded.

"Um," he started. "The . . . Reptilians. We saw them. Me and Eesha. Back home."

Natalie Pressure gasped.

"They looked human," Eesha added, "but everything

about them was weird. The way they talked and moved. It was strange."

Peacekeeper Margot turned to the woman beside her and whispered into her ear. After a moment, she turned back to Ike and company. "And where did you see these Reptilians?"

Ike looked down at his feet. He could feel his mom staring at him. "I saw footprints that looked like a lizard's, on one of my walks."

"And then we actually saw them in their human form when we were in the woods one day," Eesha added. "It was like they were looking for something."

"There's a portal there in the woods," Mixie admitted in a contrite voice. "That's how I came through." She hung her head. "I know I wasn't supposed to. I'm sorry."

Ike wanted to reach out to console her, but it was impossible. She wasn't sitting next to him. Plus, he didn't know how she would react.

"Another portal in the woods?" his mom ventured.

Ike only nodded.

"Goodness gracious," she murmured.

"Wait a minute," Eesha said. "If the Reptilians followed Ike's mom here, what were they doing on Earth, anyway? Why couldn't they just . . . come here directly and attack you? In your time?"

Peacekeeper Margot shifted in her tall seat. "I've been pondering that very question, child."

Ike saw Eesha sniff at the word *child*.

"My theory is that they were looking for unguarded portals in your fourth dimension," the Peacekeeper went on, "since they cannot breach ours."

Fourth dimension? Ike thought, dazed once again.

"We have made every precaution to deter the Reptilians from approaching space-time anomalies. Our defensive safeguards prevent them from slipping through."

She looked to Ike's mom. "But in *your* world, the space-time anomalies were . . . unguarded."

Ike rubbed his chin. Even though he knew he and his friends were in a lot of trouble, he couldn't help but be fascinated. "So," he began, "the Reptilians came to our time to find portals to bring them here?"

Peacekeeper Margot nodded once more. "We had no record of these portals before you came through. Somehow, they had never been found. Perhaps something in your time caused a rift of some sort."

Natalie Pressure raised an inquisitive eyebrow. "We discovered that the portal I came through was created by hydrogen bomb testing in the 1950s . . . at a place called the Nevada Test Site."

Ike and Eesha immediately turned to each other, mouths agape.

"The testing caused atmospheric disturbances: time loops, wormholes. Since then, we've been experimenting with time travel for decades."

She fell silent. Ike couldn't believe it. "But why?" he asked. "Why did the Reptilians want to come here?"

"Our world in *our* time has resources," Peacekeeper Margot replied. "Some of the richest in the galaxy. These valuable elements power our ships and our society. Unique protons and neutrons that are beyond your understanding. The Reptilians crave these valuable resources to make weapons."

"So," Natalie began. "You're telling me there are other species in the cosmos?"

Peacekeeper Margot chuckled. "Of course. You didn't think that Earth was the only place where life evolved, did you?"

"That's been debated for centuries," Natalie said, "but there's never been any proof."

Peacekeeper Margot leaned forward. "I think those downed Reptilian ships out there are proof. Don't you think, Pressure?"

"Yes, Peacekeeper," Natalie replied.

Ike still had so many questions for his mom and the council, but the way his mom was looking at him kept him from speaking up again.

Now Peacekeeper Margot did resemble a judge about to hand down a sentence. She steepled her fingers together. "This is all very . . . unusual."

"I didn't mean any harm," Natalie Pressure said, her voice apologetic. "I am on a mission of peace and goodwill. I'm sorry it caused such distress."

Ike had never seen his mom look so vulnerable.

"Our timeline is suffering," she went on. "War, famine. Global warming. We might be on the brink of total collapse if something isn't done soon."

The Peacekeeper paused for a moment and eyed all of them, lastly resting on Ike, who wilted a little under her intense gaze. "Your wishes will be granted, Natalie Pressure," she finally said, turning back to Ike's mother. "We have . . . resources and patents you can take back to help your people. *Our* people, I suppose I should say."

Ike's mom sighed in relief. Ike and Eesha couldn't help but smile.

But Mixie shook her head. "If I may speak, Peacekeeper, wouldn't that be messing with their future? We've always been told that interfering in the past—"

"True, Ms. Gold," Peacekeeper Margot cut her off.

"But in this case, we can make an exception. There will be pushback from some of our members, but I think we can come to an agreement that works best for both timelines."

Her colleagues seated next to her nodded in agreement. Ike wanted to know how that would work, and fortunately, Peacekeeper Margot continued.

"We have technology that can reverse the effects of climate change in your past, but it is not as simple as that."

We can stop global warming? Ike shouted in his head. *Amazing!*

"Your world *has* to change," Peacekeeper Margot insisted. "The solutions will not be easy." She held up a long, scolding finger. "Our technology can put your people on the path to repairing the planet, but it will be up to you to finish it. If not, this will all be in vain."

Natalie Pressure smiled in gratitude. "Thank you. I will not fail in this mission. From the people of your past, we thank you."

Peacekeeper Margot nodded. "You are welcome to stay and rest for a while, Specialist Pressure, as are your son and his friend."

Ike looked to Eesha and smiled, but she looked troubled.

"What's wrong?" Ike asked.

Eesha fiddled with her fingers. "I'm worried about

home. My little sister and brother and mom and dad. They've probably gone to the police or something."

"I don't think that will be too much of a problem," Peacekeeper Margot said.

Ike and his mom both cocked their heads, curious.

"Don't you remember what I told you when we first met?" Mixie said.

Eesha shook her head.

"Once you get back, you'll find that hardly any time has passed. Wormholes and time dilation both make time more . . . fluid. It's all about causality and quantum entanglement."

"What's more," Peacekeeper Margot explained, "we have the technology to . . . *pinpoint* time. The faster you travel through time, the more it slows down. We can pretty much set a point in time and then send you there."

Ike stared, dumbfounded. He couldn't wait to write all of this down in *Ike's Journal of Amazing and Fascinating Things.*

"Well, that's certainly a relief," Eesha exclaimed.

Natalie Pressure opened her mouth then closed it. And then opened it again. "Peacekeeper. Will that technology be part of the . . . solutions I bring home?"

Peacekeeper Margot stared at her. "No."

Ike's mom dipped her head in a gesture of respect.

"And *you*, Ms. Gold," Peacekeeper Margot went on, turning to Mixie. "*You* were given orders by the Peace Force that you flagrantly ignored: used an undocumented portal for time travel; entered a secure, private building; and gave your father a near heart attack, from what I've gathered. I know your mother well, and she will *not* be pleased. For the time being, you are free to go, but rest assured, there will be consequences."

Ike watched as a shade of crimson rose up Mixie's neck.

"I understand," she said softly.

The room fell quiet. Ike wasn't sure what to say or do next, but his mother decided for him.

"As for you, Ike Pressure," she said, turning to face him. "When we get home. You. Are. Grounded."

Chapter Thirty-One

Mixie was sent home to face her parents, but the Galactic Council put Ike, his mom, and Eesha up in what they called Spa-Cubicles: small rooms in a building shaped like a honeycomb. Ike was pleased to find his room had all the comforts a traveler from his time could imagine, including Virtual Sky, the holographic technology that put movies, music, and TV shows right in the room with you. He couldn't take his eyes off of it.

He thought about all he and Eesha had discovered and what they had done. It had been incredible! He still couldn't believe it. What would it be like to go back home knowing there was so much more to reality than he had thought? Would he suddenly become uninterested in the things he liked? How could he play *Shadow Goons* knowing that somewhere out there in the universe there was a Galactic Council, crazy technology like Mixie's theorem equalizer, and a spacefaring species of evil Reptilians?

Surprisingly, considering everything that had transpired, he slept well that night.

But still, he was a little worried.

We're going to have a talk tomorrow, young man. Eight a.m.

That's what his mom had said to him right before a very stern Peace Force officer had showed them all to their quarters.

And now he was quaking in his shoes. Grounded for life. Eternity. No more video games. No more walks in the woods. He and Eesha probably wouldn't be able to hang out for a while, either. Which was weird, because he finally realized that they were indeed best friends. *Strange how that works*, he thought, as he left his room and met Eesha at the elevator.

"You ready?" he asked her.

"Good morning to you, too," she said, bleary-eyed. "I'm still half asleep. I was up all night playing basketball on Virtual Sky. I beat Michael Jordan at free throws!"

Ike couldn't muster any excitement. He was too frazzled.

They took the elevator up several floors and walked down a long, white-tiled hallway to arrive at Ike's mom's room. He pressed the little round buzzer to the right of the door.

"Come in," his mom's voice piped through the speaker, in the most unfriendly tone possible.

Ike and Eesha stepped inside. Ike closed the door behind him.

His mom stood in the center of the room, hands on hips. *Military mode*, Ike thought. She always stood like this when he was in trouble.

His mother's room was a little larger than his. A window took up most of one wall, letting in warm rays of light. Everything had a clean, modern look to it, with a white semicircle couch, two lounge chairs that looked like they were made of some kind of foam, and a glass table on tripod legs.

"Sit," Natalie Pressure commanded them.

Ike and Eesha sat in the two lounge chairs. His mom remained standing. She looked tired, Ike noticed. She was probably more stressed out than he was.

"Talk," she said.

And that's what they did.

They told her about the short-wave radio and the numbers station.

Meeting Mixie for the first time and seeing the Men in Black.

The Reptilian footprints in the woods.

The word-search book where they had found clues to decipher the message.

And finally, he told her how they used Mixie's tech to sneak onto the base. Ike thought her head was going to explode.

When he finished, they sat in silence for several minutes. He felt a bead of sweat roll down the back of his neck but remained motionless. He didn't want to look at her, so he hung his head. Eesha was frozen too, not moving a muscle.

Natalie Pressure shook her head slowly. "I am so disappointed in both of you."

She didn't sound mad. She sounded exhausted.

"How could you betray my trust like this, Ike? Didn't your dad and I raise you right?"

Ike nodded glumly. He felt terrible inside. He wanted to curl into a ball and disappear, but he managed to eke out a few words. "We were just trying to figure everything out, Mom. I wanted to make sure you were safe."

Natalie turned to Eesha. "And you, Eesha. I thought you had better sense than this."

Eesha squirmed in her chair. "Are you going to tell my parents?"

Ike's mom raised an eyebrow. "Perhaps. Or not. Maybe they'll put you on The List."

Eesha's eyes grew wide. "The List? You know about it? What is it, exactly?"

"Pray you never find out," Natalie replied.

Eesha gulped.

"But," she went on, "for all the bad you've done, you acted out of a concern for me, Ike. That counts for something."

Ike finally raised his head and gave a hesitant smile.

"We'll be going back tomorrow," she declared. "I still have talks scheduled with the Peace Force and some of their scientists. There's an interview they want to film for a TV show."

"Cool," Eesha whispered, then looked sheepish and fell silent again.

"When we get back," Natalie went on, "you'll have to meet with my boss, General Davis."

Ike recalled the steely-eyed man with a chest full of medals on the army base. He shivered.

"Why?" Eesha asked.

Natalie Pressure turned her sharp gaze on Eesha.

"You'll find out."

Eesha started to chew a fingernail. "What do you mean . . . 'I'll find out'?"

Natalie Pressure smiled, but it wasn't friendly. "Because you're going to meet with him too."

Chapter Thirty-Two

Ike met Eesha in the common area of the Spa-Cubicle for lunch, while his mom spoke with the Peace Force for her scheduled interview. Just like the exterior of the building, the ceiling was honeycomb patterned, and light shone down in brilliant rays. They sat at a table in a cafeteria of sorts. Around them, several people sat at tables like theirs—working, Ike assumed, judging by the floating screens in front of them.

"I guess we can get some food here," Ike said, looking around.

"I wonder what they have to eat," Eesha replied.

"Hey, homies!"

They turned to see Mixie striding up to their table with another girl about her age. Ike was surprised to see that she was Black.

Eesha looked at Mixie skeptically. "You weren't grounded?"

"Grounded? No. I can leave the house. Mom and Dad

just took all of my tech away, including my theorem equalizer and all my gadgets. I'm pretty much a Luddite now."

"Luddite?" Eesha ventured.

"It's a person who doesn't use technology," Ike told her. "It's a word from nineteenth-century England."

Eesha's eyebrows rose in admiration. "Well, look at you, Mr. Smarty-Pants."

"Guys," Mixie started. "This is my friend Silver. Silver, meet Ike and Eesha."

Ike smiled and Eesha gave a little wave with her hand. Silver and Mixie sat down across from them. Silver wore a strawberry-red jumpsuit. Her hair, not surprisingly, was silver, styled in a pixie cut, just like Mixie's.

"I can't believe I'm talking to someone from the year 2024!" she exclaimed, studying Ike and Eesha intently.

"We can't believe we're talking to someone from the year 3000!" Eesha fired back.

Ike wanted to ask Silver a question, but he didn't know how to phrase it. He fumbled for a moment before he could get the words out. "Silver, so, um . . . the future. *Our* future. Do we ever, um, get past all the hate and stuff?"

"He's talking about racism," Eesha said bluntly.

Silver's mouth formed an O. "Well, that's a good question, Ike. Unfortunately, there are some people who still think that way."

"But they're outcasts," Mixie added. "Our society doesn't recognize them. Right, Silver?" She reached for her friend's hand and clasped it.

"Right," Silver replied. "After we learned there was other life in the cosmos, most of us started thinking of humans as one big family. One people."

"But some," Mixie added, "still didn't want to change. Stuck in the past. Ignorant."

Ike smiled. With help from Peacekeeper Margot, and knowing that society was working toward eliminating racism forever, Earth could still have a bright future.

☆ ☆ ☆

Silver used a sleek gold phone—much smaller and thinner than any phone Ike and Eesha had ever seen—to order food for everyone. There were no waiters. AI bots strolled the restaurant delivering food. "These are seaweed algae cakes with banana peppers," Silver started. "And here we have roasted cardamom pods, some briny noodles, and truffles from Mars."

Ike remembered when he and his parents went to a fancy restaurant once, and his mom ordered pasta with truffles. They were delicious—earthy and savory at the same time. "Truffles?" he repeated. "From Mars?"

"We've got hydroponic farming there," Silver said. "Lots of crops are grown that way."

Ike couldn't believe that people actually *traveled* to Mars, never mind grew food there. He licked his lips and dug in. It was all very different from what he was used to eating, but still, it was some of the best food he'd ever tasted.

Best of all was a drink called Choco-Blast. It tasted like a milkshake, but Mixie said it had more health benefits. Ike wasn't sure about that. It tasted way too sweet to be good for you.

He drank two.

☆ ☆ ☆

They lingered as long as they could, but Ike knew that now was the time to say goodbye. He wasn't looking forward to it. He really liked Mixie, and without her, their whole adventure may have never gotten off the ground. *Literally.*

"Well," Mixie said, reluctantly. "I think it's time we get ready to go."

Eesha suddenly looked very dejected.

Ike frowned. "Thanks, for, um, everything," he started. "We wouldn't have been able to come all this way without you."

"It was great to meet you, Mix," Eesha said. "You, too, Silver. Hope everything goes okay with your parents. Especially your dad."

Mixie scoffed. "He's really a big softy. Mom's the one I have to worry about."

Ike and Eesha chuckled.

There was a moment of uncomfortable silence.

"Nice to meet you guys, too," Mixie said.

Ike stood up, which seemed to be a sign for everyone else. He wasn't exactly sure what to do next, so he offered his hand for Mixie to shake.

"*Really?*" Mixie said, and then embraced him in a warm hug, which he awkwardly returned.

"I don't know if you'll get a chance to come back to our time," Eesha said, once they parted, "but if you could, it would be totally maximum."

"Agreed!" Mixie laughed and gave Eesha a hug as well. "I'll never forget you guys."

"We won't forget you, either," Ike replied.

That's when he knew his summer and his adventures were almost over.

Chapter Thirty-Three

They met his mother in the lobby of the Spa-Cubicle building early the next morning. A Peace Force official came to escort them to the Galactic Council headquarters, where the *Quicksilver* was being prepared for the return journey. Ike overheard his mom asking the official about the pilots of the Peacekeeper ships that were downed. He was glad to hear that none of them were badly injured. They all had wounds, but most of them were already healed with something called Cura-Skin.

Ike and Eesha tagged behind his mom and the peacekeeper. Neither one of them spoke, caught up in their own thoughts. Ike looked around as he walked—at the futuristic buildings, the gleaming clean streets, a blue sky free of pollution—and it almost brought a tear to his eye.

"This is our future," he said.

Eesha raised her head to the sun as she walked. "It's beautiful. And now your mom has the tech to help our world become like this one."

Peacekeeper Margot met them as they entered the building and took them to the launch site. The technology looked amazing, even though Ike didn't know what he was looking at. There were sleek crafts of silver and white; huge glass cylinders full of colorful swirling liquids; giant metal tubes being spun on some sort of centrifuge—he couldn't keep his eyes from wandering everywhere. He wanted to ask questions, but Peacekeeper Margot had a no-nonsense look about her that Ike had seen before: on his mom.

Several official-looking types huddled in the background in what looked like white lab coats. "Who are they?" he whispered.

Eesha shrugged. "Engineers? I saw them studying *Quicksilver.*"

Ike risked a glance at his mother. She looked very proud standing by Peacekeeper Margot's side. She held a silver briefcase, which Ike imagined was full of hope for Earth's future. He smiled inside. She'd done it. She traveled in time and was going back to tell the tale. *And so are we*, he thought to himself.

Peacekeeper Margot turned to Natalie Pressure, who stood at attention, ramrod straight. "With these tools from our shared future," she began, "I wish you peace and goodwill toward humanity. It is not enough to think only of the here and now, but for generations to come. Give your people a legacy and an Earth that is thriving and safe."

Ike's mom raised a hand to her brow to salute.

"Your craft is ready," Peacekeeper Margot finished with a wave of her arm.

"Thank you," Natalie said. "Thank you all. This means so much to us. To our shared planet Earth. We will never forget."

Peacekeeper Margot turned to her left and raised her hand. Ike watched as a man in a white lab coat, one of the engineers, stepped up to a long table and began to turn a bunch of knobs on something Ike couldn't quite see. He looked like a DJ about to spin some EDM.

But that's not what happened.

A flash of blue and white light erupted in midair.

"Wow," Ike exclaimed.

"What is that?" Eesha whispered.

"It's a new portal," Peacekeeper Margot said. "Set to accurately pinpoint the time you left. It's been under guard these past two days. Once you go in, we will close it forever."

Ike blinked. The light morphed into a massive oval hole, with blue lightning dancing around its edges, a hazy white tunnel swirling within its depths. He got dizzy just looking at it.

Peacekeeper Margot turned back to them. "Ready?"

And with that, Ike and Eesha followed his mother to *Quicksilver*.

Ike's stomach pitched in anticipation. He was about to fly through time with his mom! How cool was that?

Inside, the craft was small, but there was just enough room for all of them to lie very close to one another. Ike's mom fiddled with a display of lights and dials. The sound of switches being clicked made him all the more nervous. Eesha closed her eyes and took a big breath.

Ike felt a buzz of adrenaline race through his body. The lights on the ceiling of the craft began to blink rapidly.

"All strapped in?" his mom asked.

Ike and Eesha checked their buckles, and then stared back up at the ceiling. A display screen suddenly appeared—a ghostlike pattern of whirlpools, triangles, and vortexes. "Wow," Ike said softly.

Natalie Pressure spoke into a small device, cataloging the date and time. "Quicksilver STAV ready for launch," she said.

Ike felt something shift, like *Quicksilver* was charged with some kind of energy. He couldn't see it, but he felt the fine hair on his arms standing up. His ears began to ring.

And then, he closed his eyes.

Chapter Thirty-Four

The trip home was nothing like his departure with Eesha and Mixie. One moment Ike had closed his eyes, and the next he was opening them again and it was over. He was reminded of when he got his tonsils taken out and woke up not even remembering the procedure.

"We're home," he heard his mother call. "Everyone okay?"

"Yeah," Eesha said, unclicking her safety belt.

Ike followed suit. "Well, that seemed fast."

"I want you both to take a deep breath before you stand up," Natalie said. "Give your body a moment to readjust. Count to ten."

Ike released a heavy breath. And then another. His ears popped. He counted aloud, in unison with Eesha.

"Okay," his mom said. "Let's go." She stood up, opened the hatch, and helped Ike and Eesha out . . . to find a crowd of people in uniforms waiting. Ike recognized one of them.

"Pressure," General Davis said, taking in Ike and Eesha. "What in jumpin' Joseph . . . !"

Ike had no idea who Joseph was or why he was jumping.

"General Davis," she addressed him, giving a salute. "Mission accomplished. I, uh . . . have a debrief for you."

General Davis continued to look at Ike and Eesha with steely eyes. "I bet you do, Pressure. I bet you do."

Ike gulped.

"First thing we need to do is get you all to a decontamination center . . . ASAP," General Davis ordered.

Without so much as a word, four military police escorted them to one of the many nondescript buildings on the base, where they all had to shower with a special stinky soap that smelled like ammonia. But that wasn't all. A doctor looked inside their mouths and ears. They had blood drawn, which made Ike wince. Eesha didn't seem to mind. She watched the little tube filling up and said, "Wow. Cool." Ike felt like a lab rat. Once the exams were done, they were all given clean boring-looking gray sweat suits.

They were led to a room with hard folding chairs and a metal table—all military issue, which meant nondescript and plain. The scent of the ammonia filled the room.

Eesha wore a scowl and looked as if she would rather be anywhere else than there.

After Ike's mom explained Ike's and Eesha's involvement, General Davis studied them with fresh eyes. "Well," he said. "We definitely have a FUBAR situation right here, Pressure."

Ike and Eesha exchanged uncertain glances.

"Fubar?" Ike repeated.

"Fouled up beyond all recognition," his mother clarified.

Ike gulped.

General Davis and a woman in civvies asked them several questions. There was another man there from INSCOM as well, taking notes as Ike and Eesha recounted everything that led to their mission to the future. They were particularly interested in Mixie's theorem equalizer. Unfortunately, Ike and Eesha couldn't tell them much about how it worked.

After they were finished, silence filled the room. Ike felt a bead of sweat at his temple. It was hot in the room, and the air seemed to hang like a dead weight.

"Outstanding!" General Davis boomed, making them jump. "Truly outstanding."

Ike's mom raised an eyebrow. "Sir?"

The general stood up and began to slowly pace in the small room. He looked at Ike's mom for a long moment.

Ike saw her shrink in her chair a little.

"Only one thing to do," he said cryptically.

Ike closed his eyes. Eesha gnawed her fingernails. "The List," she whispered. "I'm going to be put on The List."

"The only list you'll be on is for some kind of . . . junior espionage team," the general replied. "Not sure of the name yet. We'll give it to the guys and gals over in communications. Maybe . . . Kidcraft, like statecraft, you know?" He rubbed his chin. "Or . . . Undercover Kids."

Natalie Pressure looked to the INSCOM man, who only shrugged. She turned back to the general. "Sorry, sir. I don't follow. What exactly are you suggesting?"

"These kids broke the law, Pressure."

Ike squirmed in his seat.

"But in doing so," he continued, "they exhibited skill, bravery, and a noble search for the truth. Everything we stand for in the United States Armed Forces. They'll be disciplined, for sure. But I think we might have a place for them once they've done their time."

"Time?" Eesha squeaked.

"Community service," the general replied.

Ike breathed a sigh of relief, although he still worried what this community service would be like.

"Let me get this straight, sir," Natalie started. "My son and his friend spied on us—even using some kind of futuristic nanoparticles to enter restricted areas of the base—and you want to . . . recruit them?"

"That's about right. We'll start them out on something low-key and not too dangerous. Maybe taking a look at some of those encrypted messages we got over that new numbers station."

Ike and Eesha turned slowly to stare at each other. Ike couldn't believe what he was hearing. "Sir, you want us to work for you? For the military?"

"Affirmative," General Davis replied. "You kids have some resources that today's military is underutilizing. The FaceToks and the—whatchamacallit—YouBook."

Ike tried to hide his amusement. He knew if he had looked at Eesha, they'd both burst out laughing.

General Davis turned to Ike's mom. "That is, of course, with your approval, Pressure, and the parents of Miss Webb here."

Ike had seen his mother in a lot of different situations, and she always remained cool and levelheaded. But this time, she seemed at a loss for words. "Yes, General Davis," she finally said. "If you think that would be a good way to go, I'm on board."

Now Ike couldn't hide his excitement. He grinned from ear to ear. And finally, his mom smiled at him.

One of the general's assistants brought in a beige

old-school landline phone with a long cord and set it in front of Ike's mom. "Go ahead and call your husband, Pressure," General Davis said. "I'm sure he's waiting for your return."

Ike listened as his mom talked to his dad for a moment. He was embarrassed. It was kind of mushy.

"I need to call home, too," Eesha said quietly. She was still worried, even though Mixie and Peacekeeper Margot had told them that they wouldn't lose any time. "I'm sure *some* time has passed. I mean, I left the twins all alone and now I'm here."

Ike's mother smiled. "I'll do it for you. Your parents are going to find out one way or another about this. Plus, you'll need their approval if you're going to . . . work for us."

Eesha exhaled.

That was nice of her, Ike thought.

"Outstanding," General Davis exclaimed again, when Ike's mom hung up the phone. He looked once more to Ike and Eesha, studying them for a long moment. "Okay, first things first. Before we really recruit you, you're gonna need another physical."

Ike groaned.

Chapter Thirty-Five

"Ike Pressure! Ten-hut! Get down here! Early bird gets the worm!"

Ike rolled over in his bed. He glanced at the alarm clock: 7 a.m.

He sighed and stared up at the ceiling. Even helping secure Earth's future wasn't enough to let him sleep in.

As he stumbled his way downstairs, an odd smell rose up to greet him.

"Bacon!" he shouted.

He rushed into the kitchen to find his dad cooking eggs. A plate of bacon sat on the table. His dad turned away from the stove. "I told your mom every kid deserves a treat now and then."

"Thanks, Dad," he said, sitting down. "Mom."

He picked up a nice crispy slice and bit into it.

Crunch.

He closed his eyes and swooned.

"Just don't get too used to it," his mom warned him, as

he reached for another. His dad spooned a heaping amount of cheesy eggs onto his plate. So far, this whole morning was going a lot better than he would have ever thought.

His mom and dad sat down to eat as well. His father had the same as Ike, while Natalie had avocado on toast and a slice of fresh honeydew melon.

"So, Mr. Time Traveler," his dad started. "You still have chores. First, we're going to trim the hedges. And then later, I want you to help me clean out the basement for my home gym."

"Aha," Ike said, lost in his own bacony fantasy. "Sure, Dad."

After they were finished, they sat at the table a while longer. Ike wanted to ask his dad something, but he was apprehensive. Finally, he just blurted it out. "Dad, you knew about Mom's mission, right?"

Mr. Pressure looked to his wife, who nodded. He turned back to Ike. "I didn't know all the details, but I knew what she was doing. We share everything, Ike."

"Why didn't you ever tell me?"

Natalie set down her toast. "Ike, that mission was top secret. Only spouses were allowed to know, and even then they had to have a security clearance. We didn't want to keep it from you, but that's the way it had to be."

"The numbers," he said cautiously. "We picked them

up on the old radio. How . . . how did that happen?"

His mom glanced at her husband and then Ike. "We started using numbers stations to avoid cyber-interference and data leaks. We never thought that anyone would pick up on the signal. And even if they did, they'd need the word-search book we were using to crack the code."

"We did, though," Ike said hesitantly.

"And that's my fault," his mom replied. "It was a one-in-a-million chance that a woman working on a top secret project would also have a son with a short-wave radio and a very curious mind."

"So it was just luck, then?"

"Well, luck and your and Eesha's combined intelligence. I'd forgotten all about that old radio. And even when I saw you with it, I convinced myself that there was no way you were using it. I should have known better."

"Guess you won't be using that method again."

His mom shot him a warning look. He gulped down his bacon and reached for another piece, but she swatted his hand away. "That's enough, Ike. Save the rest for a BLT sandwich for lunch."

Ike meekly drew his hand back. He had another question to ask. "Mom, I know you said I was grounded, but before that happens, can Eesha come over? We haven't had time to talk since we got back."

Natalie looked at her son and shook her head. She smiled, though, which was a good sign. "You two really *are* best friends now, huh?"

Ike shrugged. "Guess so."

She turned to her husband, who held up his hands. "Don't see why not."

"Okay, Ike," she started. "Just today. After that, you have to do your time."

"Thanks, guys."

He stood up quickly . . . and snatched a slice of bacon and rushed upstairs.

☆ ☆ ☆

Eesha looked around Ike's room curiously, taking in his posters, rock collection, and other stuff. "So, this is where all the nerdery happens."

"Yup."

She picked up a stack of papers on his desk.

"Hey!" Ike said defensively from where he sat on the bed.

"*Ike's Journal of Amazing and Fascinating Things,*" she read from the cover.

"I just printed that out. It's a collection of stuff I thought was interesting."

Eesha flipped through the pages. "Pretty cool. Look at the size of this mushroom! That's wild!"

"I know, right?" Ike replied.

Eesha set the book down, picked up a rock, turned it over, and set it back down.

"So, what did your parents say about your trip to the future?" Ike asked.

Eesha sighed and plopped down at Ike's desk. "Your mom must have said something, because they didn't ask a lot of questions. I don't even know what she really told them, but I'm not bringing it up."

"Isn't it weird that we were only gone for a short amount of time?" Ike said.

"Well, if you think about the time dilation and blah, blah, blah, it all makes sense."

They both laughed at her imitation of Mixie's scientific jargon.

"I miss her, though," Ike reflected.

"Me, too."

There was a moment of silence.

"So, we went to the future and came back with nothing," Eesha said. "Doesn't seem quite right, does it?"

Ike looked at her skeptically. "Really? Nothing? How about getting to see an alien race in a battle with my mom? Or drinking Choco-Blast? Or . . . flying around in a spaceship?"

"Guess you're right," she reconsidered.

"And," Ike went on, "the most important thing is that we helped my mom. And she came back with tools to help Earth's future. What could be better than that?"

"Some of those invisible nanoparticles?"

Ike grinned. "Yeah. That would be cool."

"Could you imagine," Eesha said, "going to school with that and messing with everybody's heads?"

"I'd use it on all the bullies."

"I'd use it at basketball practice." Eesha rubbed her hands together gleefully. "I'd be making three-pointers, and no one would know where they were coming from!"

She peered around the room for anything else to discover. "The radio," she said all of a sudden. "Where is it? Have you listened to it since we got back?"

"No," Ike said.

"Let's see it."

Ike retrieved the radio from under the bed and plugged it into the socket near his desk. "Can you believe this old radio started this whole thing?"

"I know," Eesha replied. "Maximum."

Ike turned it on.

Static floated from the speaker.

And then, a child's voice:

"Baa, baa, black sheep,
Have you any wool?
Yes sir, yes sir,
Three bags full."

Ike and Eesha turned to look at each other, mouths wide.

But the message was not over.

"3, 7, 9, 4, 6 . . . Foxtrot. 7, 5, 3 . . ."

"Here we go again," Eesha said.

A rush of adrenaline raced through Ike's body.

And then he picked up a pencil and began to write.

Read more by Ronald L. Smith!